Essential Irish
MYTHS AND LEGENDS

Gill Books

Hume Avenue, Park West, Dublin 12

www.gillbooks.ie

Gill Books is an imprint of M.H. Gill & Co.

Copyright © Teapot Press Ltd 2026

ISBN: 978-1-8045-8487-3

This book was created and produced by Teapot Press Ltd

Text by Joe Potter

Illustrated by Renia Metallinou

Designed by Tony Potter

Printed in the EU

This book is typeset in Futura and Optima

All rights reserved.

No part of this publication may be copied, reproduced or transmitted in any form or by any means, without permission of the publishers.

To the best of our knowledge, this book complies in full with the requirements of the General Product Safety Regulation (GPSR). For further information and help with any safety queries, please contact us at productsafety@gill.ie

A CIP catalogue record for this book is available from the British Library.

5 4 3 2 1

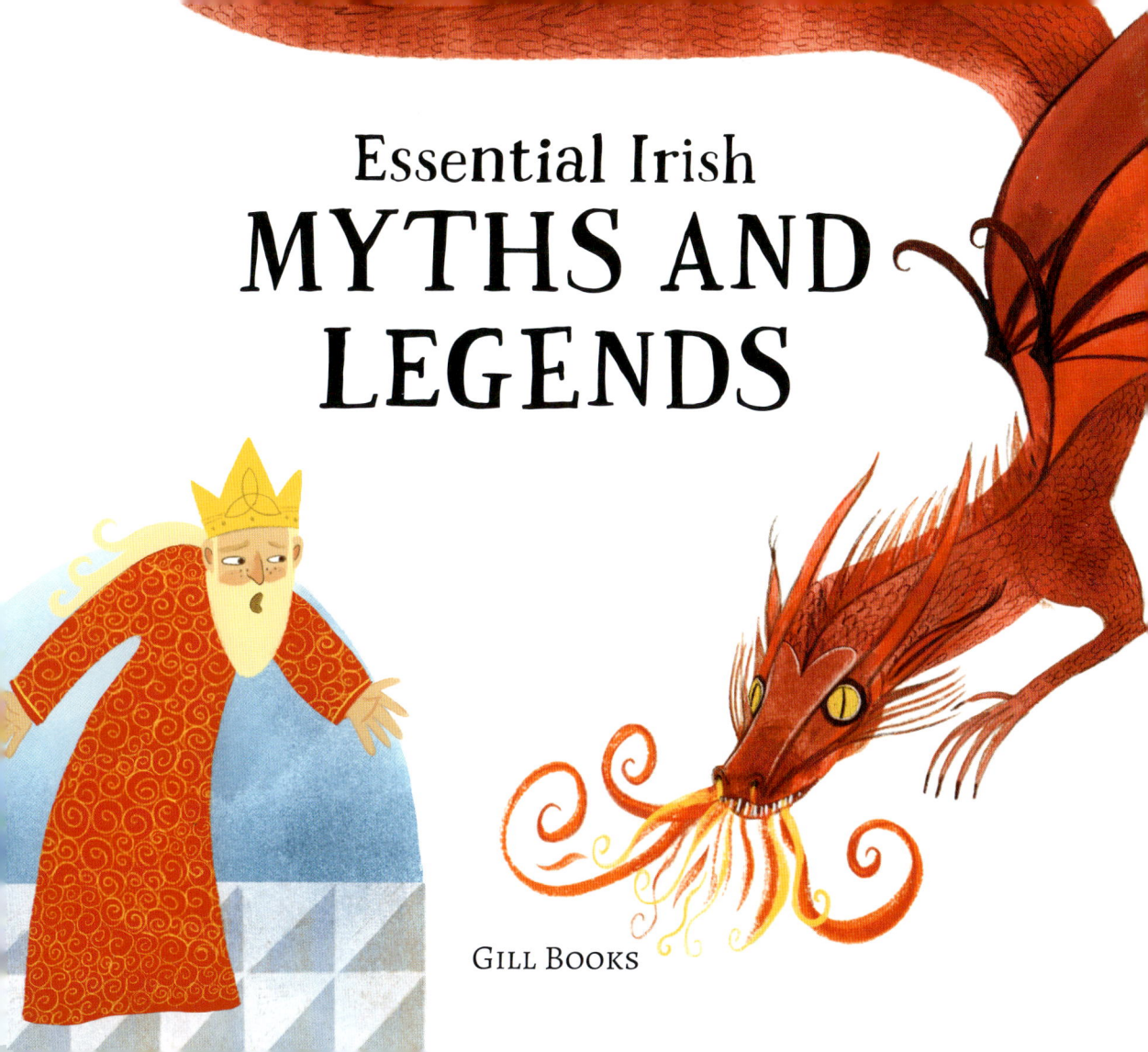

Essential Irish
MYTHS AND LEGENDS

GILL BOOKS

Contents

6   Introduction
8   The First Battle of Mag Tuired
18 The Cattle Raid of Cooley
30 Fionn Mac Cumhaill and the Salmon of Knowledge
44 Oisín and Niamh in Tír na nÓg
58 Deirdre of the Sorrows
70 Fionn and the Dragon
82 Setanta Becomes Cú Chulainn
94 The Coming of Lugh, God of Light

108 The Death of Cú Chulainn
118 The King with the Donkey Ears
130 The Birth of Fionn
144 The Giant's Causeway
158 Diarmuid and Gráinne
170 The Lazy Beauty and Her Aunts
184 The Twelve Wild Geese
198 The Gardener's Sons
208 The Children of Lir
222 Pronunciation Guide

Introduction

Ireland's ancient stories arise from a landscape where history, myth and imagination have always existed side by side. Long before stories were written down, the people of Ireland shaped their understanding of the world through spoken legends – tales carried by poets and storytellers, told beside hearth fires, and woven like a tapestry into the hills, lakes and seashores of the land itself. These legends are not merely fantasies; they are mirrors of human experience, reflecting courage and tragedy, love and loss, pride and humility, and the eternal struggle between light and darkness.

Within these pages are gathered some of the greatest tales of the Irish tradition. Here march the gods and heroes of the Tuatha Dé Danann in *The First Battle of Mag Tuired and The Coming of Lugh, God of Light,* where divine power clashes with chaos. The heroic age unfolds through the life of Cú Chulainn, from *Setanta Becomes Cú Chulainn* and *The Cattle Raid of Cooley* to the poignant ending in *The Death of Cú Chulainn*. Alongside these stand the adventures of Fionn Mac Cumhaill, whose wisdom is won in *Fionn Mac Cumhaill and the Salmon of Knowledge,* whose birth and battles shape the Fianna, and whose world touches wonder in tales of dragons, giants and enchanted shores such as *The Giant's Causeway.*

Love and sorrow flow just as strongly through these legends. *Deirdre of the Sorrows, Diarmuid and Gráinne,* and *Oisín and Niamh in Tír na nÓg* tell of passions that defy kings, time and fate itself. Stories of transformation and moral lesson – *The King with the Donkey Ears, The Children of Lir, The Twelve Wild Geese,* and the quieter folk tales of humility and kindness – remind us that magic often carries a price, and wisdom may arrive in unexpected forms.

Together, these legends tell of Ireland's mythic past, inviting you to step into a world where heroes walk among gods, and every story leaves an echo that still lingers today.

The First Battle of Mag Tuired

Long ago, Ireland was a land of many peoples. It was said that the gods themselves once walked upon her hills, plains and shores. Among the tales they told is the story of the First Battle of Mag Tuired, when two great peoples, the Fir Bolg and the Tuatha Dé Danann, fought for the soul of the island.

The Fir Bolg had lived in Ireland for many generations. Once they had been slaves in distant lands, forced to labour in servitude, carrying heavy bags of clay upon their backs. Through toil they became hardened, and when they finally escaped and returned to Ireland, they divided the island into five provinces and ruled with order and pride.

Their king was Eochaid mac Eirc, a man of stern face and strong arm. Under him the Fir Bolg knew peace, though it was a peace sharpened by vigilance, for they feared what might come across the sea.

Far away, across the northern seas, the Tuatha Dé Danann prepared to claim a new home. They were not like ordinary mortals. They were a people steeped in magic, druidry, and craft. Their smiths forged weapons of terrible brilliance, their poets spoke words that shaped reality, and their healers could mend bone and flesh with herbs and charms unknown to mankind.

They carried with them four treasures from the northern cities:

- The Stone of Fál, which rejuvenated the worthy.
- The Spear of Lugh, which blazed like lightning and never missed its mark.
- The Sword of Nuada, from which no one could escape once it was drawn.
- The Cauldron of the Dagda, which produced food in perpetuity.

At their head stood Nuada, tall, fair, and commanding. He bore a king's strength, but also a king's wisdom. His people adored him, for he ruled not with tyranny but with fairness. The Tuatha came to Ireland's shores, clouded in secrecy. They cloaked themselves in a great mist of enchantment that hid their landing. Some say the Fir Bolg awoke one morning to see clouds resting on the western hills and when the clouds lifted, the Tuatha stood there, armed, radiant and terrible to behold.

Nuada sent envoys to the Fir Bolg with this message: 'We are the Tuatha Dé Danann, children of the goddess Danu. We ask of you half of Ireland, to share as our home. If you refuse, we will take what the gods will grant us by strength of arm.'

When the message was brought before King Eochaid, he scowled.

'Half of Ireland? We bled for every inch of this land. We carried clay upon our backs and won this country from stone and thorn. Not for all the gods of heaven will we divide it now.'

His champions beat their spears upon their shields in agreement. The Fir Bolg would not yield.

The messengers returned to Nuada, who bowed his head gravely.

'So be it. Then on the plain of Mag Tuired shall this be decided – whether Ireland belongs to the Fir Bolg, or to the Tuatha Dé Danann.'

The two hosts marched to Mag Tuired, a broad, level plain in Connacht, surrounded by wooded hills. For days the ground trembled with their coming. The Fir Bolg marched in iron ranks, shields glinting, banners snapping in the wind. The Tuatha came in silence, cloaked in enchantments, their druids chanting spells as they walked.

The Fir Bolg numbered many thousands, and their war cries cut the morning air. The Tuatha were fewer, but each was a master of craft or magic, and they carried weapons no mortal smith could make.

For four days they faced one another across the plain, each side sending forth champions to test the other.

On the first day, single combats filled the field. Sreng, the mightiest warrior of the Fir Bolg, came forward wielding a massive iron club. His blows could shatter shields like twigs. Against him came Nuada himself, sword in hand. Their duel was fierce; sparks flew as iron struck enchanted steel. At last, with a crushing stroke, Sreng sheared through Nuada's arm at the wrist, severing it from his body. Blood spattered the ground, and Nuada staggered back, gasping.

The Tuatha rushed forward to bear their king away. The Fir Bolg roared in triumph, and Sreng lifted the bloody weapon high. Yet the battle did not end, for Nuada, though maimed, refused to yield.

On the second day, the druids of both sides cast enchantments. The Tuatha called up storms of wind and sheets of flame, while the Fir Bolg's druids countered with darkness and thunder. The plain itself seemed to groan with the weight of their spells.

On the third day, the hosts clashed in earnest. Blades rang, spears flew,

and the cries of the dying rose up to heaven. Warriors fell in heaps, the plain turning red beneath their feet.

On the fourth day, King Eochaid mac Eirc himself entered the fray. He was a warrior of terrible strength, and he smote many of the Tuatha. But at last, in the heat of battle, he fell beneath their blades. With his death the heart of the Fir Bolg broke, and their army scattered.

When the fighting ended, thousands lay dead upon the plain. The Fir Bolg were shattered, their king slain, their champions broken. Only

Sreng and a small band survived, retreating to the western edges of Ireland.

The Tuatha, though victorious, mourned their losses. Nuada, their beloved king, had lost his hand, and by the law of their people, no blemished man could rule. Though he had led them to victory, he was forced to lay down the crown.

Nuada bowed his head and said: 'Though my spirit is strong, my body is marred. I will not bring dishonour upon the Tuatha Dé Danann. Another must rule in my place.'

Thus began a sorrowful time, for the Tuatha, despite their triumph, found themselves troubled by questions of kingship and destiny.

But before the Tuatha claimed Ireland, Nuada offered Sreng one final gift.

He summoned him and said: 'You fought with honour and nearly struck me down. I will not see your people destroyed utterly. Take a fifth of Ireland, if you wish, and dwell there in peace.'

Sreng, weary and grieving, shook his head.

'I cannot rule in defeat. But I will lead my people west, to Connacht, and there we will live, though our glory is gone.'

And so it was. The Fir Bolg retreated to the edges of Ireland, and the Tuatha Dé Danann claimed the island as their own.

The plain of Mag Tuired was littered with bodies, a grim reminder of the price of sovereignty. The Tuatha built great mounds over their dead, raising cairns that stand even today. They sang laments for their fallen and gave offerings to the gods.

Nuada, though beloved, was no longer king. A new ruler was chosen: Bres, son of a Fomorian father and a Tuatha mother. But his reign would prove dark and bitter, leading to the great Second Battle of Mag Tuired, when the Tuatha would clash not with mortals, but with the monstrous Fomorians themselves.

For now, however, Ireland belonged to the Tuatha Dé Danann. The Fir Bolg were broken, their power ended. The gods of Danu had claimed the land, and their names would echo in song and story for generations to come.

The First Battle of Mag Tuired

The Cattle Raid of Cooley

Long, long ago, when the sword was mightier than the pen, the rulers of Ireland held their dominion with an iron fist. The north was in the grip of the great Conor Mac Neasa, King of Ulster. To the south, the land of Connacht was clutched by Queen Maeve and her husband Ailill.

Maeve and Ailill were powerful rulers and power hungry. But more than this they yearned for greatness, to stand taller than any man or woman alive, including each other. Their rivalry was infamous, fervent and vicious. If Maeve killed a stag, Ailill would hunt a wolf, if Ailill built a tower, Maeve would build a castle and on and on it went …

One autumn morning Maeve clanked proudly into the great hall at breakfast. Her subjects gasped at the sight of her — for she was wearing the most beautiful armour anyone had ever seen, including Ailill. The breastplate shone with bronze, with intricate swirling patterns and great jewels that glinted at the shoulder and collar. Caught in the morning light she was nothing less than dazzling.

'Need I say it? This is surely the most splendid amour in the land!' She gazed imperiously up at Ailill, 'I dare say it makes your armour appear as a pile of scrap dear husband. In fact I rather think it outshines anything in your possession.'

Ailill lounged on a huge oaken chair, trying to appear nonchalant but there was cold fury in his eyes. 'Yes, dear it is most beautiful indeed, but no suit of armour could hope to

compare to this.' Ailill clicked his fingers – eyes still fixed on his wife. At once a servant hurried off and returned with a large object covered in a cloth. With one motion he swept off the fabric, revealing a portrait the likes of which had never been seen. It was of Ailill himself and though he was depicted most handsomely it was the object in his hand that incensed Maeve most. He had been painted holding a pineapple, a gift from a king in a tropical land far away, which had sent the castle into great excitement the previous month.

'Did I neglect to give you a bite dear wife? It was the most delicious thing I have ever tasted. I would compare it to something for you but it really was beyond anything you could imagine.'

Maeve's face screwed up in fury, but she rallied almost at once, clapping her hands sharply. She had foreseen the battle and had a few tricks up her sleeve. Two ladies swept into the hall holding a flowing gown. The ladies at the tables craned their necks and stood up for a better look. Ailill could find no criticism. The gown was of the most delicate shimmering silk, embroidered in patterns so intricate they might have been stitched on by fairies.

'Four women laboured for a year to weave this gown,' she said. 'Your painting pales in comparison, even with that stupid pineapple. And what's more I have a new horse!' And at her word the most stunning mare came trotting into the hall – coat shining almost as highly as her armour. The king's subjects all clapped, admiring the glossy hair and gleaming flanks.

Privately Ailill felt it made his colt look like some weary cart horse but his smile did not falter, 'Most impressive dear wife, I have to admit this time you have bested me.'

The court all gasped, and Maeve let out a derisive laugh. 'Let it be known throughout the land who is the victor, who is the …'

Ailill raised his voice, 'Oh there was just one more thing my love; could everyone come outside for moment.'

Curious, everyone got up from their seats and followed Ailill to a private field behind the castle. Maeve reluctantly brought up the rear. The crowd were all fighting to get a better look but all stood aside as Maeve came striding through. What on earth could be so impressive?

Maeve stopped dead. Standing in the field was the finest bull she had ever seen. Not only was it twice the size of any normal bull. But none had seen one more muscled, more ferocious, more majestic. And there was something else, something in the shine of its white hair, almost glowing, like magic.

'This,' Ailill said carelessly, 'is Finnbhennach, my prize bull. There can be no question, it is greater than any bull, any horse, any gown, or any suit of armour.'

Maeve stood there aghast. There was simply no denying it, the bull was beyond anything she possessed. Hot pride rose in her chest and she stormed away without another word.

When she was back in the castle she screamed for her advisor, 'Mac Roth, come here!'

From the far end of the hall, a tall man came running. 'At your service, my queen.'

Maeve lowered her voice, 'Tell me true, is Ailill's white beast the greatest to be found in all Ireland?'

Mac Roth grinned. 'No, there is one greater. In Ulster, old Daire of Cooley owns a monster of a bull: the Brown Bull of Cooley. He is feared and admired across the land.'

Maeve clapped her hands. 'I must have him. Go at once to Daire. Offer him fifty, a hundred of our best cows in exchange. Offer him land, gold, anything, I must have that bull!'

Mac Roth and his men rode hard to Ulster. When they reached the castle, Daire greeted them warmly enough but hostility erupted almost at once. He politely refused all Mac Roth's offers. 'I'm sorry dear boy, no land, gold or cow is greater than my bull, my answer is no.'

Mac Roth sighed, 'Be reasonable Daire, I have offered you fair and if you do not, Maeve will simply take the bull by force.'

A fury rose in Daire. 'You dare to meddle with Daire. I have the might of King Conor Mac Neasa behind me. Bring your army Mac Roth. You will fall upon us like water!'

When Mac Roth returned empty-handed Maeve's fury equalled that of Daire. 'Gather every able warrior!' she cried. 'We march for Ulster at once.'

When King Conor Mac Neasa heard of Maeve's march north, he sent out his famed Red Branch Knights. But along the road, Maeve ordered her sorcerers to cast a terrible sickness upon the Ulster warriors. One by one, they fell to the wicked spell – all except the famed warrior Cú Chulainn, who was untouched.

Maeve's army pressed onward, but in the woods and along the hillsides, Cú Chulainn hunted them. His sling cracked like thunder, and with each stone, another Connacht warrior fell. If he caught a straggler, his spear was swift and merciless.

The losses mounted until Maeve feared her army would be destroyed. She sent a messenger to Cú Chulainn with promises of gold, land and honours if he would join her side.

'I will not fight for you,' Cú Chulainn replied. 'But I will give you this mercy – I will face your warriors one at a time.'

The next day, on the banks of the River Dee, Cú Chulainn stood alone before Maeve's army. He was only seventeen, slender and clean-faced. Maeve's men laughed at the sight. But one by one they came forward – and one by one they fell. By the end of the day, the ground around him was littered with a hundred bodies.

Maeve called for her greatest warrior, Ferdia. But Ferdia shook his head. 'I will not raise my sword against Cú Chulainn. We were foster brothers. It would be a great sin to harm him.' Maeve coaxed, threatened and bribed. At last she whispered a lie: 'He calls you a coward, hiding behind my skirts.' Ferdia's pride flared. He armed himself and strode into the shallows of the Dee to face his friend.

For three days they fought – blades ringing, shields splintering, neither gaining the upper hand. At night they sent for food, drink and herbs to heal their wounds, so that each might fight at his best the next day.

On the fourth morning, as they clashed again, the recovered Red Branch Knights appeared on the far bank and began to cheer. Cú Chulainn turned his head for a heartbeat – and in that heartbeat, Ferdia's blade swept across his chest.

Cú Chulainn fell to his knees, his sword slipping into the water. Ferdia raised his weapon for the killing blow – but a comrade on the bank flung a spear into the river. Cú Chulainn snatched it, drove it upward, and struck Ferdia through the heart. Ferdia collapsed into his arms. Tears filled

Cú Chulainn's eyes as he cradled his dying friend. There was no joy in the victory, only grief.

The Red Branch Knights charged into Maeve's army, which broke and fled. But in the chaos, Maeve slipped away with a small band, rode to Daire's land, and took the Brown Bull by stealth. When she saw the beast, her breath caught. Twice the size of Ailill's white bull, with a dark, rippling hide and muscles like carved stone, he was every bit as splendid as Mac Roth had promised.

She returned to Connacht in triumph, ordering that the bull be locked safely in a strong pen. 'Guard him well,' she commanded. 'If the Ulstermen come, defend him with your lives.' But the Brown Bull was restless and enraged at being taken from his home. His deep bellow echoed through the castle grounds and Finnbhennach, hearing the challenge, charged from his own pen.

Servants scattered as the two beasts met. Maeve herself hurried to watch, her eyes alight. 'Now we shall see which bull is the greater!'

All night they fought, their horns clashing, hooves pounding, breath steaming in the cold air. Finnbhennach was quick, darting aside from

the Brown Bull's heavy charges, but in the end his speed failed him. The Brown Bull caught him with a mighty thrust, and Finnbhennach fell lifeless to the ground. Ailill hung his head as his wife cheered.

The Brown Bull, still mad with rage, smashed through the fence and galloped for home. But the fight had drained him. Before he had gone far, he stumbled, collapsed and died on the road to Cooley.

Maeve's cheers died in her throat and Ailill turned to her with a thin smile. 'I think in the end dear, no one was the victor here.'

Fionn Mac Cumhaill and the Salmon of Knowledge

Long ago, when stories were newly sewn and wisdom was worth more than jewels, there lived a boy named Fionn Mac Cumhaill. In years to come, he would lead the Fianna, fight great battles, and have his name sung across Ireland. But before wielding a sword, a person must learn to wield their mind.

Fionn's parents understood this well and they worried for him. Their son was energetic, agile and strong but he was also impulsive and hot headed. He yearned to join the Fianna and fight at once. They felt if they weren't careful their son would not live to become a man. They decided that before their son learned the arts of war, he must learn the ways of thought. But how to make their son see as they did?

One morning Fionn came to his parents full of resolution, 'I am leaving

to join the Fianna! Don't cry mother, my mind is made up!'

Fionn's mother raised her eyebrows, 'You may need a sword if you are to join up dear.'

Sensing a rage building up in his son, and also an opportunity, Fionn's father spoke, 'You shall have a sword my son but you must go on an adventure to find something in exchange.'

Fionn perked up measurably, 'An adventure! Absolutely! What do you desire father? The feather of an eagle? A wolf fur?'

'No, nothing like that … I wish you to bring me … wisdom.'

'Wisdom?'

'Just so. There is a old man famed from one end of the island to the other – a poet and scholar called Finnegas. He is the wisest man alive. He is said to understand the language of birds, the patterns of the stars, the turning of the seasons and mysteries more ancient still.'

'Oh yes,' chimed in his mother, 'His words are like bright coins tumbling from a treasure chest and all who hear scrabble to grab them. Go and find him my son and when you return with wisdom you shall have your sword.'

'You've got it, I'll come back with more wisdom than you know what to do with!'

Fionn set off at once. The way was long and he was still little more than a boy, but Fionn's determination was a wind at his back. For three days and nights he crossed hill, valley and dale. He slept in ditches and tree hollows but every morning brought forth fresh fervour. Even when it rained on the second day his spirits were not dampened for he had the promise of his sword to bear him. At last he reached the wide dancing waters of the River Boyne. There, beneath the shade of a great chestnut tree, was a most odd fellow hopping about on the bank. He was barefoot, with long white sweeping robes and a beard to match. Coming closer Fionn saw he was yanking a fishing rod back and forth with a fish. The fish appeared to be putting up rather a good fight.

'Here let me help you!' But by the time Fionn reached the old man the line had snapped.

'Damn! Wriggled away again!'

Fionn surveyed the old man uncertainly. With his popping eyes and enormous beard he really did look a bit crazy, 'You must be the great Finnegas?'

'Well I don't know if I must be! But you are Fionn Mac Cumhaill.'

'How on earth do you know that?'

'Your mother sent a raven to tell me you were coming.'

'Oh,' said Fionn, a little disappointed.

'Being all knowing is not wisdom young man. Indeed it is wise to know that! For that is why you have come, no?'

'Yes, oh great one. I have traveled many leagues to find you. I beseech you to teach me wisdom. I will do anything you require of me in return.' Fionn sank to one knee and bowed. When he looked up he saw an amused smile playing about Finnegas' lips.

Finnegas chuckled 'Wisdom is a slippery fish. She leaps from your grasp, wriggles free and leaves you wet and bewildered. Not everyone has the patience to catch her.'

'I have patience enough wise one.'

'Maybe you do, maybe you don't, that remains to be seen.' Finnegas considered the boy, for he had already seen a flash into the boy's future, as soon as he'd first looked in his eye. He saw greatness in this boy's destiny.

'But greatness and goodness seldom go hand in hand.'

Fionn stood frowning, 'What?'

Finnegas' smile broadened. 'I will strike you a bargain. I will teach you what I know in exchange for a little … housework.'

'You're on!' cried Fionn. He followed Finnegas excitedly up the hill towards his little cottage. He was used to housework, his mother made him scrub all the time. But nothing could have prepared him for Finnegas' house. It was without a doubt the messiest, dirtiest, most ramshackle hovel that Fionn had ever seen – clothes crumpled in heaps, dishes piled high and crusted, papers scattered like autumn leaves, dust gathering thick enough to write one's name in, and every corner strung with spiders' webs.

'You want me to clean this?'

'Oh yes,' said Finnegas striding away, 'and I want supper every day too.'

And so their arrangement began. Each day Fionn scrubbed, scoured, wiped, dusted and washed. At times he felt as though he were fighting a many-headed Hydra. Every time he cleaned something, another fouler, smellier horror would pop up. But however slow the progress, it was worth it for every afternoon Finnegas would teach him. He found a curiosity for thought that he had never experienced before.

Despite Finnegas' mad appearance, he was quite as wise as the rumours said. He spoke of constellations and the way birds foretold the weather, of far-off lands and the old heroes, of stories and songs until Fionn could repeat them word for word. Yet the more the boy learned, the hungrier his mind became. His questions grew sharper, and at last, there came a day when even Finnegas could not answer them all.

'Is there no way to know everything?' Fionn asked.

The old poet grew thoughtful. 'There is a way,' he said at length. 'And it lies in this very river.'

'Really?' Fionn jumped to his feet. 'I'm an excellent swimmer. I'll jump in to fetch it!'

'Fetch, fetch? No, no boy, it must be caught. It is like wisdom itself, it can only be gained with patience. Sit down, I shall tell you the tale. We sit – as you see – in the shade of an oak tree. Legend says that once every 10,000 years this tree bears a single magic chestnut, a chestnut that carries all knowledge. When it last fell the chestnut was gobbled up by a salmon who instantly gained all the knowledge for himself.'

'So we have to wait 10,000 years?'

'No, no! You simply have to catch and eat the salmon and then the knowledge will be yours!'

'I'll catch it Finnegas, I'm great at fishing.'

'Hmm … I have been trying for years to no avail but there is no harm in trying!' Finnegas plucked up his rod and handed it over to Fionn. The boy sat on the bank, casting and waiting, but he caught only trout, pike and eels. After two days of patient sitting, he threw the rod down in frustration. 'That fish is nothing but a story!'

For a while Fionn sat in silence eating the fallen chestnuts around him and gazing into the waters.

'Boy!' Fionn turned to see Finnegas running down the bank toward him, 'What are you eating?'

'Chestnuts Finnegas.'

Finnegas struck his head with his palm, 'Stupid, stupid! So simple. Ha ha!' And he bent double snatched up a chestnut and attached it to the fishing line.

'Just because I am wise, does not mean I cannot be stupid! Sometimes when your head is in the clouds you forget what is right in front of you.' The old man took a deep breath and cast the line into the river, 'It never occurred to me to simply fish with chestnuts.'

The float bobbed in the water and a great excitement rose in Fionn. It was after twenty minutes, when his expectancy was starting to wane, that it happened. The line went taut. 'Help me Fionn!' Fionn grabbed up the rod as well. The fish was powerful, thrashing beneath the water. The line could break at any moment. So they reeled it in ever so gradually. They gave a little and reeled a little – two steps forward and one step back. Finally they were close enough and Finnegas cried, 'Now!' and they yanked the fish out of the water. When it broke the surface the scales shimmered, dazzling with colours no ordinary fish possessed. For this was

no ordinary fish. As it flopped on the bank Finnegas gave a huge whoop.

'At last! It is mine! The Salmon of Knowledge! Quickly Fionn, make a fire and cook this prize!'

The boy rushed to obey, though he could not help but feel a pang of disappointment that it was not he who had made the catch. Finnegas, however, was firm. 'This is my fish, boy. Do not take so much as a bite, for its gift can be given only once.'

While the poet went to gather more firewood, Fionn turned the fish over the flames. At one point, the skin began to blister and spit hot juices. A drop landed on the boy's thumb, burning it. Instinctively, he popped it in his mouth to ease the sting – and in that instant, something stirred inside him.

When Finnegas returned, he studied the boy's face. 'You have tasted it.'

'No!' Fionn protested. 'Only – I burnt my thumb and sucked it to stop the pain.'

The old man closed his eyes for a moment. 'That is enough. The gift is yours now. Eat the rest, for it will do me no good.'

So Fionn ate, but when the last mouthful was gone, he frowned. 'I feel no different.'

Finnegas sat silent, mourning the loss of what he had sought for so long. Yet at last he said, 'When you wish for wisdom, put your thumb to your mouth again, as you did before.'

Fionn obeyed – and in a heartbeat, the world opened. He knew the turning of the tides, the paths of the stars, the speech of the wind in the trees. He saw far into the past and far into the future. Everything Finnegas had taught him was there, and much, much more.

'I understand,' Fionn whispered. 'I see everything.'

The poet nodded gravely. 'Then your time with me is over. Go and make your own path. Use well what you have been given.'

Fionn left the banks of the Boyne with the gift that would guide him all his days. He would become a warrior and a poet, the leader of the Fianna, and the wisest man in Ireland.

As for Finnegas, he returned to his verses and his fishing, content – or nearly so – to be the second wisest man in the land.

Fionn Mac Cumhaill and the Salmon of Knowledge

Oisín and Niamh in Tír na nÓg

Back when Ireland was still young and the world seemed bright and new, there lived a warrior named Oisín. He was a man destined for greatness. How could he not be? His father was none other than Fionn Mac Cumhaill, the legendary leader of the Fianna, Ireland's guardians and champions. Like his father before him, Oisín grew into a man of courage, strength and poetry. He was admired not only for his skill in battle but also for the beauty of his songs and tales.

One bright morning, Oisín and the Fianna were hunting deer near Lough Leane. After a long chase, they rested by the water's edge, laying their spears aside. Their hounds lapped happily at the water. None of the men were talking. The only sound was their breath, until a sharp intake broke the rhythm. One of the men stood and pointed across the lake, 'Who is that?'

   Riding around the bank was a figure unlike any they had ever seen – a woman, on a snow-white horse. Both so breathtaking they might have galloped down from heaven. True silence had fallen now, even as the woman approached, for the horse's hooves struck no sound upon the earth, gliding as though it rode on air.

   As she drew nearer, the Fianna beheld her radiance. She was the most beautiful woman their eyes had ever gazed upon. Her golden hair streamed to her waist, shining as if woven from sunlight. Her skin was pale and perfect, like polished ivory, and her eyes gleamed blue as sapphires set in silver. A light surrounded her, soft and glowing, as if she carried the very dawn within her.

The warriors fell silent, awestruck, until Oisín himself stepped forward, unable to resist the pull of her presence.

'Fair maiden,' he stumbled, as though the words were not his own, 'W-where have you come from? You can be no mortal woman. Surely I speak to one of the Otherworld?'

When she spoke, her voice was a melody most gentle but more rousing than any song the men had ever heard. The sound filled them with a beauty so astounding it was almost frightening.

'I am Niamh of the Golden Hair,' she said. 'Daughter of

the King of Tír na nÓg, the Land of Eternal Youth. You are Oisín, son of Fionn, warrior and poet of the Fianna.'

'Yes,' Oisín gasped, 'How do you know me?'

'You are known to many in the Otherworld. I have come across sea and sky to find you.'

At her words, the men turned to Oisín, astonished. He himself felt his heart tremble, for he knew at once that destiny had called. 'How can I serve you lady?' he said, bowing his head.

Niamh smiled, her beauty dazzling as sunlight on water.

'I come with a gift and an invitation. In Tír na nÓg there is no sorrow, no pain and no death. Our people never age, and every wish of the heart is fulfilled. Will you ride with me, Oisín, and share eternity in the land of youth?'

'Why would you offer this to me?'

Niamh gave a blink that held an eternity, 'You feel us in your world in the falling of snow, in the smell of rain, in the sound of ocean. We experience mankind in our world. You could not understand, but your call sings to me in far more beauty than the vision you see before you now.'

Oisín turned for a moment to his companions, to the Fianna who were his brothers in arms. He thought of his father, of Ireland's hills and forests, of the home he loved so dearly. Could he leave it all behind? Yet when he looked again into Niamh's radiant eyes, his answer was already written.

'My lady,' he said, 'I will go with you. Gladly do I choose to ride at your side.'

Niamh reached down her hand, and Oisín leapt lightly onto the back of her snow white horse. Turning to the Fianna, Oisín called, 'Fear not, dear friends! Though I ride away today, I will return to you. This is not farewell forever.'

The horse reared, then galloped forward – swift as the wind, silent as a dream. The Fianna watched their comrade fade into the distance, their cheers mingling with the rush of the wind.

As they rode, Oisín gazed back one last time at Ireland's green fields. 'I shall miss it dearly,' he whispered.

'Wait until you behold Tír na nÓg,' Niamh said, her eyes shining. 'There you will find endless joy: forests forever in bloom, orchards heavy with golden fruit, streams that sing with laughter, and skies filled with light. Music and poetry fill the air, and sorrow is a word unknown.'

The horse skimmed across land, its hooves never quite touching earth. When they reached the sea, it did not pause but galloped across the waves as though over glass. A path of sunlight stretched before them, guiding their way. Time itself seemed to dissolve – perhaps they rode for moments, perhaps for years – until at last the shores of Tír na nÓg rose before them.

It was a land beyond imagining. Fields of flowers stretched further than the eye could see, mountains glittered with crystal peaks, and lakes shone brighter than silver. Birds of every colour darted through skies of perpetual dawn. Everywhere they rode, smiling faces welcomed them, faces of unearthly beauty. Golden light bathed all things, filling the heart with peace.

At the palace gates stood the King and Queen of Tír na nÓg. They greeted Oisín warmly, marveling at their daughter's joy. 'You are most welcome here, son of Fionn,' the king declared. 'In this land you may have whatever your heart desires. No grief, no age, no death shall ever touch you.'

As Oisín dismounted, his feet touched the ground, and in that instant, every shadow of care seemed to vanish. He felt lighter, stronger, as though he had been reborn. Niamh took his hand and whispered, 'This is your home now, as it is mine.'

That night, a feast was held in Oisín's honor. Never had he seen such wonder. The halls glittered with starlight, music filled the air, and tables overflowed with delicacies. Wine flowed from golden fountains, and laughter rang like bells. The celebration lasted for days, and when it ended, Oisín knew he had truly entered a world of eternal delight.

Soon after, he and Niamh were wed. Their love was fierce and true, and they spent their days in perfect happiness. Oisín hunted in green forests, composed poems by shimmering lakes and feasted by starlight. Every evening, he and Niamh sang together until sleep carried them away.

Yet sometimes Oisín wondered if man was meant for paradise. There was no battle to fight, no barrier to overcome. He had arrived and the man in him longed for a journey. At the great feasts he told stories of Ireland, of his father Fionn and of the Fianna. The people of Tír na nÓg listened eagerly, but for Oisín, the tales stirred bittersweet longing.

Time in Tír na nÓg flowed differently. Days and nights slipped past like shadows. What seemed a few short years to Oisín was in truth three hundred years in the mortal world. At last the weight of longing grew too heavy to bear. One evening, he turned to Niamh.

'My beloved,' he said, 'I have all that a man could wish for, yet my heart aches for Ireland. I must see my people once more, if only for a moment.'

Tears shone in Niamh's eyes. 'If you go, my heart will grieve, yet I cannot hold you against your will. But hear me, Oisín: take my white horse, and remember this above all – do not touch the ground of mortal Ireland. If you set foot upon it, you can never return to me.'

'I swear it,' Oisín promised. 'I will not dismount.'

The next morning, he kissed Niamh farewell and mounted the white horse. With a cry it leapt forward, flying across the sea as it had before. The winds howled, waves surged, and in a heartbeat Ireland's green hills came into sight.

But Ireland was not the land he remembered. The Fianna's halls lay in ruins. Castles had crumbled, fields were changed and the faces of the people were strange. Not a soul knew Fionn Mac Cumhaill or the warriors of old. Everywhere he rode, Oisín searched in vain for a trace of his kin.

Weary and sorrowful, he entered the Valley of the Thrushes. There he saw men struggling to move a heavy boulder from the road.

'Help us, good sir!' they cried.

Oisín trotted over, wanting to perform some small duty in his homeland but he remembered Niamh's warning. Leaning down from the saddle, he pushed with all his strength. The stone shifted, but as it did, the strap of his saddle snapped.

Oisín tumbled to the earth. In the instant his body touched the soil of mortal Ireland, the white horse gave a mournful cry and vanished into the air.

And Oisín – once youthful and strong – was transformed before the men's eyes. His hair grew white, his skin withered, his limbs trembled with age. Three hundred years crashed down upon him in a heartbeat.

The men, horrified and pitying, carried him to St Patrick, the wise holy man of the new faith. There Oisín told his tale of Tír na nÓg, of his love for Niamh, of the promise he had broken.

Patrick listened with compassion, yet could offer no help. 'I cannot return you to that world, my son,' he said gently.

Tears welled in Oisín's eyes. 'Then tell me at least – what of the Fianna? What of my father, Fionn Mac Cumhaill?'

Patrick placed a hand on his shoulder. 'They are long gone, Oisín. But their memory lives, and through you, their stories endure.'

So Oisín, frail and weary, spoke through the night. He told Patrick of battles fought, of hunts and feasts, of laughter by the fire. He spoke of Fionn not only as a leader but as a father: of lessons shared, of love given. He spoke, too, of Niamh and the land of eternal youth, of beauty beyond words.

At last, when his strength was spent, Oisín lay back and closed his eyes. His final breath left him, carrying his soul to join his father and the Fianna in the halls beyond this world.

Oisín never returned to Tír na nÓg, yet the tale of his love and loss lived on, passed from generation to generation. And so long as it is told, the names of Oisín and Niamh will never fade.

Deirdre of the Sorrows

Long ago, in the kingdom of Ulster, there lived a royal storyteller in the court of Conchobar named Fedlimid mac Daill. He told eager crowds of ancient gods and heroes. Even kings prized the wonder of his words. When his first daughter was born, Fedlimid carried the newborn child to the wisest druid in the court, asking for a prophecy.

'Cathbad old friend, I must know my daughter's future. Will people tell stories of her one day?'

The druid, placed a hand upon the infant's brow. But almost at once he recoiled, as if burned.

'Yes, they will, dear Fedlimid, but it will not be one you will want to hear,' the druid said gravely. 'This girl is marked by sorrow. She will grow to be the fairest woman in Ulster, but her beauty will bring ruin and sorrow. Many men will fall by the sword because of her.'

A murmur swept the court of the Red Branch. The Knights cried out that the babe should be killed at once, lest the prophecy come true. But Conchobar, ever greedy and cunning, rose to his feet. Only one word had registered with him of the druid's prophecy – beauty. If she was indeed to be fairest in all Ulster he would have her for his bride.

'Kill a helpless child?' he scoffed before his men. 'No, no. I have a better plan. Let her be hidden away, guarded and unseen. When she is grown, she shall be my queen.'

Fedlimid launched himself before the king and begged for his daughter but Conchobar was pitiless, 'It is for the child's own good Fedlimid. Take her away!'

And so the child, Deirdre, was taken deep into the forest and entrusted to Leabharcham, a wise poet-woman. In her care, Deirdre grew up in seclusion, far from the world of men.

As the years passed, Deirdre's beauty unfolded like the dawn. Her hair shone golden as the morning sun, her skin gleamed pale as snow and her eyes were the deep, brilliant blue of the summer sea. Yet her life was lonely. Leabharcham was kind and learned but she was a guardian, not a friend. A friend … the first thing Deirdre had ever desired but in time her desire grew for more than just a friend.

One night, a fabulous dream came to her. In it, she saw a young man – lithe with careless curls falling about such eyes that could only exist in a

dream. She woke with her heart racing
and told Leabharcham of the vision.
'And he was singing to me, such a voice
you never heard.'

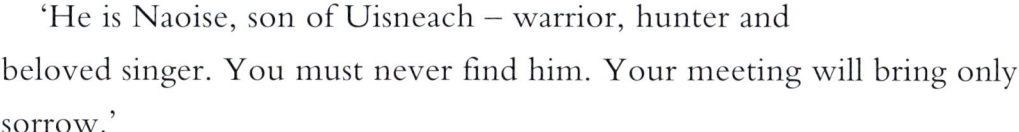

Leabharcham grew pale, 'Child,' she said,
'I know the man of whom you speak.'

'You know him? Who is he? Where can I find him?'

'He is Naoise, son of Uisneach – warrior, hunter and beloved singer. You must never find him. Your meeting will bring only sorrow.'

But Deirdre wasn't listening, 'Where can I find him? You must bring him to me.'

'No!' Leabharcham cried. ''Tis too dangerous. You are promised to the king. To love another will doom you both.'

But Deirdre begged without ceasing, her loneliness gnawing at her like hunger. At last, worn down by love and pity, Leabharcham relented. She

sent word to Naoise who rode off at once. Deirdre's beauty was known across Ulster and would have sent any man galloping at her word.

The moment Deirdre and Naoise met, their eyes locked, and love bloomed fierce and unyielding. Deirdre's heart knew its truth: she could never love Conchobar. There was only Naoise.

'We must flee,' she whispered. 'We must go far from Ulster, far from the king's reach. I would rather live in exile with you than be queen in chains.'

So Naoise, together with his brothers Ardan and Áinle, fled with Deirdre into the night. They wandered first across Ireland, seeking refuge, but none dared receive them. Word travels faster than hooves. Conchobar had learned of this betrayal with Naoise and his word was vengeance. At last, they sailed across the isles of Scotland, where they found peace for a time.

There, on a green island, Deirdre and Naoise wed. They hunted, fished, sang songs beneath the trees, and for a while their days were full of joy. Yet even in happiness, Deirdre's heart trembled. She knew the king would not rest until he had claimed her. And she was right.

Back in Ulster, Conchobar brooded, his pride wounded by her flight. Years passed, yet his jealousy and desire did not. They deepened – like an old spell – more potent with every passing day. At last one of his spies located them on the isle of Alba. He sent the noble warrior Fergus mac Róich as messenger to Alba, bearing words of false forgiveness.

'Come home,' the king's letter said. 'All is forgotten. Return to Ulster, and no harm shall come to you.'

When Naoise heard this, he longed to believe it.

Fergus was known as an honourable man; surely, if he swore to escort them safely, no treachery could befall them.

But Deirdre's gift of foresight stirred within her. She dreamed of three birds carrying drops of honey in their beaks, followed by drops of blood. 'This journey,' she told Naoise, 'will end in death. I see it as clear as the moon in water.'

But Naoise's brothers longed for home and their own families. And Deirdre sensed that Naoise too was beginning to yearn for Ireland. Often she caught him staring out over the sea to his lost homeland, with a look of heartbreaking sorrow in his eyes. Guilt quieted her better judgement and finally Deirdre agreed to return.

When they landed on Ulster's shore, a nobleman delayed Fergus with an invitation to feast. Bound by honour, Fergus could not refuse. Thus Deirdre and the sons of Uisneach were left to continue alone.

As they neared Eamhain Macha, Conchobar sent Leabharcham to spy on them. When the old nurse saw Deirdre, her heart ached with mingled joy and grief. Leabharcham rushed to her, embracing her as a daughter.

Quietly she whispered:

'Do not trust the king. Take refuge with the Red Branch Knights tonight. There you may yet find safety.'

When she returned to Conchobar, Leabharcham lied. 'The years have not been kind to her Lord. Once a beautiful flower, the petals have fallen and withered. She is not worth your trouble.'

But the king was too sly for her. He sent another spy, a foul man named Glenna, who peered through a window and saw Deirdre laughing as she played chess with Naoise. Enraged, Naoise hurled a chess piece and struck the spy's eye out – but Glenna escaped to report the truth.

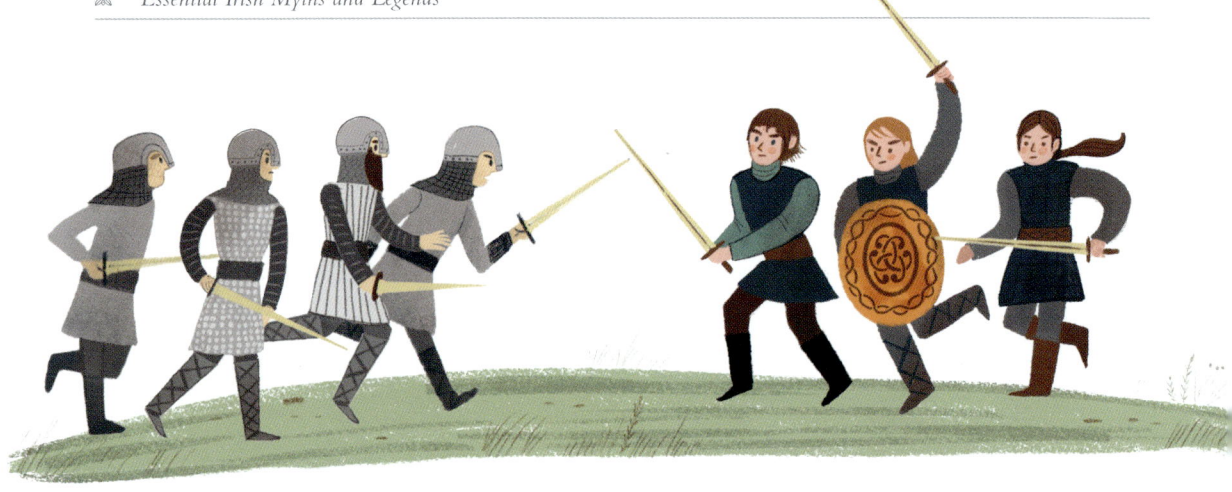

'More radiant than ever!' he cried to Conchobar. 'It was worth losing an eye to behold her!'

Conchobar's lust and fury boiled over. He gathered his soldiers and laid siege to the Red Branch House, where Naoise and his brothers sheltered with Deirdre.

The sons of Uisneach fought bravely, striking down wave after wave of the king's men. Their skill was unmatched, and for a time it seemed no force could conquer them. Conchobar, desperate, turned to Cathbad to cast a spell, but the old man was unwilling, for he feared for the brothers.

'No, no dear Cathbad,' said the king with a maniacal glint in his eye, 'I just want my bride. I promise, I shall not kill the brothers.' Well, he would not. Conchobar was always careful about how he phrased things.

Reluctantly Cathbad cast a spell that made the warriors feel as though they battled through a raging sea. The strength drained from their limbs, their swords slipped from their grasp, and at last they were overwhelmed.

Conchobar strode into the hall, his eyes fixed on Deirdre. 'The spy spoke true,' he sneered. 'You are still as fair as the prophecy foretold. You will be mine now.'

But first he sought vengeance on her beloved. 'I will give his weight in gold to the man who kills these traitors!' At last, Maigne Roughhand, son of the King of Norway, stepped forward, with his sword at the ready to do the king's bidding.

Deirdre fell to her knees, begging for mercy, but Conchobar's heart was iron.

'Kill me first,' pleaded Áinle, the youngest, 'for I cannot bear to see my brothers die.'

'No, me first,' cried Ardan.

But Naoise said, 'Strike us all together, with one blow, that none may live to mourn the other.'

And so it was done. With a single swing of his sword, Maigne beheaded the three brothers.

Deirdre's wails of grief pierced every heart but Conchobar's. Numb and broken, she made no resistance when he dragged her away. 'We will go back to my bedchamber at once. Perhaps I shall mount Naoise's head on my wall. Would you like that?'

But Deirdre's spirit was unbroken. As the chariot carried her from the battlefield, she looked upon the earth where Naoise's blood still stained the grass. She knew she could never be Conchobar's bride.

With one sudden motion, she threw herself from the chariot, dashing her head upon a rock. Death came swiftly to poor Deirdre and all Conchobar's triumph at once turned to ashes.

He buried Deirdre at Eamhain Macha beside Naoise and his brothers. In malice, he had stakes driven deep into the earth between their graves, so that even in death the lovers would be divided.

But the gods – or perhaps the earth itself – took pity. From Naoise's grave and Deirdre's, two trees began to grow, tall and strong. Their branches reached upward and outward until at last they twined together in one inseparable embrace.

Thus the prophecy was fulfilled. Deirdre's beauty brought ruin and sorrow, yet also a love so enduring that not even death, nor a king's cruelty, could sever it.

Fionn and the Dragon

After Fionn mac Cumhaill had eaten of the Salmon of Knowledge he spent several more years with old Finnegas. Apart from fishing the river dry, they spent their days sparring intellectually. Finnegas threw topic after topic at Fionn but finally he had to admit it: 'Off into the world dear boy, there is nothing more I can teach you.' Although Fionn was sad to leave his master he knew he was right. The world was waiting for him. It was time to fulfil his true destiny – to become a hero.

So Fionn left the quiet banks of the Boyne and wandered across Ireland, seeking adventure. He journeyed north to Malin Head, where the sea breaks itself against black cliffs, and south to Kinsale, where the gulls wheel over green waters. He strode through forests and across bogs, slept under stars and in the doorways of strangers' homes.

But though he sought, he found no great deeds to test his strength. His life on the road was solitary, filled with silence and small tasks: helping farmers mend fences, chasing away wolves from flocks, listening to old women tell stories by the fire. It was not enough for Fionn. His blood burned for more – for a challenge that would make his name echo down the ages.

One morning, as he walked a stony road, he spied a band of chieftains and soldiers riding in formation. Their banners streamed in the wind, their spears gleamed in the sun. Hope leapt in Fionn's heart, and he ran forward to greet them.

'Good morrow, men!' he cried. 'Tell me, what is your quest?'

The riders slowed. One of the chieftains broke free of the throng.

'No quest. We travel to Tara for the festival of Samhain. The great assembly is near.'

Fionn's face fell. Samhain was a time of peace – six weeks during which no sword could be drawn in Tara, no blood spilled. He had longed for a monster to slay, or a battle to fight. Still, feasting and music had their pleasures.

'May I join you on the road?' asked Fionn.

The chieftain gave a strange smile. 'If you wish to risk it.'

Fionn frowned. 'Risk what?'

Another soldier answered in a hushed voice, 'Tara is cursed. Every Samhain, an evil demon comes upon the city.'

'What sort of demon?' Fionn pressed.

The man's voice trembled. 'A fire-breathing dragon. Aillén mac Midhna – the Burner. One of the Tuatha Dé Danann, a creature of the underworld.

Nine years in a row he has flown to Tara on Samhain night, lulled the people with his music, and set the city aflame.'

A third soldier spoke, his voice nearly breaking with fear: 'We are doomed! Doomed to watch him burn our homes and halls again.'

Fionn's brow furrowed. 'And why have the Fianna not slain this monster? Are they not the bravest warriors in Ireland?'

The soldier looked weary. 'Because Aillén plays his magic harp, and all who hear it fall asleep. Magicians have tried to resist. None could withstand it.'

'I will kill him,' Fionn said boldly.

The soldiers all laughed. 'And how will you fight when you are snoring like the rest of us? No ordinary man can touch him.'

Fionn only smiled. For he was no ordinary man.

By the time they reached Tara, the sun was setting. Samhain had begun. The great hill of kings shimmered with hundreds of fires, torches and lanterns. As Fionn entered, he saw people dancing in the streets, making offerings of food and trinkets for the wandering spirits. But beneath the songs and laughter lay fear. Mothers clutched their children tightly. Horses stamped and snorted uneasily. Men's eyes flicked often to the darkening sky.

Near one bonfire, Fionn overheard people singing a desperate chant:

> *Samhain, Samhain, let the spirits reign,*
> *Oh mercy we ask from you, Aillén.*
> *Take our gifts and our golden spoils,*
> *But leave our Tara free from toils.*

Fionn's jaw tightened. Samhain was meant to be a joyful time, when the veil between worlds grew thin and the living welcomed the dead. But here in Tara, fear had hollowed the festival.

He strode at once to the great hall, where King Cormac mac Art feasted with nobles and warriors. The Fianna sat among them, led by the stern-eyed Goll mac Morna – the very man who had slain Fionn's father years before. As Fionn entered, Goll's gaze fixed on him, something like recognition flickering in his eyes.

Fionn marched straight to the high table.

'Who dares approach so boldly?' asked the king, looking down with amusement.

'I am Fionn, son of Cumhal,' he declared.

The hall fell into silence. All eyes turned to Goll.

'I have heard,' Fionn continued, 'that a demon plagues your halls.'

The king nodded wearily. 'Nine years running, Aillén of the Flaming Breath has burned Tara on Samhain night. None can withstand him. What of it?'

'I will slay him,' said Fionn, his voice ringing.

Laughter broke out around the

hall. The king himself smiled, shaking his head. Fionn was tall and broad, but still beardless, his youth plain.

'And for what price?' asked Cormac with a smirk.

Fionn's eyes flashed. He looked directly at Goll mac Morna. 'If I succeed, I will be leader of the Fianna, as my father was before me.'

Gasps rippled through the hall.

'Done,' said the king carelessly. 'Slay Aillén, and you may have what you ask.'

That night, while others feasted, Fionn patrolled the ramparts. Already men were yawning, their heads drooping as faint, unearthly music drifted on the wind. The notes were sweet and sorrowful, weaving dreams of green meadows and gentle seas. Fionn's own eyes grew heavy.

Suddenly a hand gripped his arm. A soldier stood there, holding a strange spear carved with runes, its head dark with a hidden fire.

'I am Fiacha, once your father's friend,' he said. 'For his sake I give you this spear of enchantment. It has the power to break any spell – if you can unlock its secret.'

Before Fionn could thank him, Fiacha swayed, collapsed and fell into a deep sleep. The music thickened. The demon was near.

Fionn bit down on his thumb, the very thumb that had tasted the Salmon of Knowledge. In a flash of insight, he learned the spear's secret. He pressed its head to his brow. At once the drowsiness lifted, and the music could no longer touch him.

All around him, the people of Tara slumped in enchanted sleep. Only Fionn remained standing.

From the dark clouds, a vast shape emerged – Aillén mac Midhna, the Burner.

The demon descended with a roar, his red-scaled body glistening in the firelight, wings vast as sails, eyes like molten gold. His maw gaped wide, and a jet of flame poured forth, searing the stones of Tara. Stables blazed. Market stalls exploded into fire. Iron warped and melted.

But wherever Aillén breathed, Fionn raced after, smothering flames with his cloak, dousing them with water, refusing to let the city burn.

The dragon turned, snarling in fury. Who was this youth who defied his fire, who did not sleep beneath his song? His wings beat the air, sending gusts that toppled wagons. His music swelled louder, desperate, but the spear's magic shielded Fionn.

Then Aillén wheeled in the sky and plunged toward him, jaws yawning to swallow him whole.

Fionn did not flinch. He waited, steady, until the demon's throat loomed before him. Then with all his strength, he hurled the enchanted spear.

It struck true, piercing beneath a scale into the tender flesh. Aillén shrieked, writhing, his body convulsing as fire spewed wildly from his mouth.

Fionn rushed forward. With a mighty stroke of his sword, he severed the monster's head. The dragon gave one final roar, and then lay still.

Silence filled the castle grounds.

Slowly, the sleepers stirred. One by one, they awoke, blinking in confusion. They expected to see Tara in ashes, but the city still stood. Then they saw Fionn, standing in the courtyard, holding aloft the severed head of Aillén the Burner.

A great cheer rose, echoing through the night.

The king himself came forth, eyes wide with wonder. 'You have done it!' he cried, clasping Fionn's hands. 'You have saved Tara. Ask what you will – it is yours.'

Fionn's gaze turned to Goll mac Morna. 'Our bargain. I will be leader of the Fianna.'

The king nodded solemnly, 'So it shall be.' All eyes turned to Goll. For a long moment he stared at Fionn. Then slowly, he bowed his head. 'I accept you,' he said, his voice low but clear. 'You have done what no man could do. You are truly our leader.' And he knelt before Fionn.

One by one, the warriors of the Fianna stepped forward and knelt as well.

And so it was that Fionn mac Cumhaill became leader of the Fianna, as his father before him. From that night onward, he would lead them to glory, and his name would be remembered forever in Ireland.

Setanta Becomes Cú Chulainn

In the old days of Ireland, when heroes walked the land and the Otherworld lay close to hand, there was born a boy unlike any other. His name was Setanta. Some whispered that he was not wholly mortal. They whispered that he was kin to Lugh, God of Light. Others said he was no mere son but the very incarnation of Lugh himself, sent to tread the green hills of Ériu in human form.

Whether these whispers were true or only the gossip of awe-struck neighbours, none could deny that greatness dwelt in the boy. His lineage stretched into high places. His uncle was none other than Conchobar Mac Nessa, mighty king of Ulster and lord of the Red Branch Knights, the most renowned warriors in the land.

Conchobar kept within his fort at Eamhain Macha a company of boys called the Macra. They were no ordinary boys, for they were trained in

the arts of war as much as in the games of youth. On their playing field they hurled and wrestled, sparred with sword and spear, and learned the discipline of warriors while still in their first years. These were the seedlings from which the Red Branch would one day draw its stoutest oaks. To join the Macra was to set one's foot upon the road of glory.

Setanta longed with all his heart to join them. Every day he pestered his mother with the same plea.

'Mother, let me go to Eamhain Macha,' he begged. 'Let me join the Macra. I am swifter than any boy in Dundalk, stronger than all of them, and you yourself have said I am the bravest.'

His mother would smile sadly, for she knew the fire that burned in her son's heart, but she would shake her head.

'You are too young, my child. A warrior must learn patience before he learns battle. A man who cannot wait cannot lead.'

But the boy's spirit was restless, like a hawk straining against its tether. He held his tongue for a year, trying to master the patience his mother spoke of. When his birthday came, she asked what gift he desired.

Setanta straightened, his eyes bright with resolve.

'Mother, I have waited a year in silence. I have learned patience, as you told me. Now grant me my wish: let me go to my uncle's fort. Let me join the Macra.'

Deichtine looked long into her son's eyes. He was still young, but the determination blazing there was not something she could extinguish with denial. Though her heart ached at the thought of parting, she nodded, 'You may go. But know this, my son: a warrior does not cling to his mother's hand. You must walk there alone.'

And so, with nothing but his hurley stick and his sliotar, Setanta set off on foot for Eamhain Macha. The road was long, stretching across miles of meadow and forest. Yet Setanta made it a game. He would strike his sliotar ahead with his hurley, chase after it at full speed, and strike it again before it touched the earth. Again and again he sent it soaring forward, never once letting it fall. In this way he tested his speed, his accuracy, his endurance, until the days passed in a blur of motion.

When at last the flags of Eamhain Macha rippled before him on the horizon, Setanta's heart leapt with joy. Here stood the fort of the Ulster king, his uncle, the very place where his destiny awaited.

Below the high walls of the fort, Setanta saw a band of boys playing at hurling. Their game was fiercer, faster, more ruthless than anything he had ever witnessed in Dundalk. Their shouts rang across the field like the cries

of warriors in battle. Without hesitation, Setanta ran forward and caught their sliotar mid-flight. The Macra froze. This stranger had dared to join their game unbidden. Fury kindled in them. With one mind, they turned their anger on Setanta, flinging their spears in challenge. But Setanta was no ordinary boy. He snatched up a shield from the ground and caught the flying shafts upon it as though it were child's play. With blazing eyes the Macra rushed him, but Setanta met their charge with unmatched swiftness. He ducked and spun, struck and parried, until he had bested them all.

Above in his chamber, King Conchobar, who had been playing chess, was roused by the uproar. He leaned from his window and thundered: 'What is this racket? Who dares disturb the peace of Eamhain Macha?'

The Macra hung their heads in shame, but Setanta stood tall and called back:

'I am your nephew, Setanta of Dundalk. I have come to join the Macra.'

The king narrowed his eyes, studying the boy. All around lay the Macra, panting and battered, while this newcomer stood unscathed, 'Did you fight my whole company alone?'

'I did, my king,' said Setanta.

Conchobar's face softened into a smile. 'Then you are worthy indeed. Come, nephew, it is my honor to welcome you.'

And so Setanta was admitted into the Macra. In short time he proved himself the most gifted among them, swiftest at the hurling, fiercest in mock battle, tireless in spirit. The other boys admired him even as they resented his prowess, for none could deny his greatness.

One season later, a feast was declared. Not far from Eamhain Macha lived Culann, the king's blacksmith, whose forge provided swords and spears for Ulster's warriors. Wishing to honour his lord, Culann invited Conchobar and his knights to a banquet.

On the evening of the feast, as Conchobar prepared to depart, his eyes fell on Setanta, who was playing hurling with the Macra, 'Setanta!' the king called. 'Come with me tonight. You are my bravest pupil, and I would have you at my side.'

Setanta ran to him at once, bowing low. 'It is my honour, uncle. But I beg leave to finish the game first. It would not be fair to leave my fellows one man short. I will come after you, for I can run as fast as any horse.'

The king laughed at the boy's boldness and agreed. Off he went with his knights, leaving Setanta to play a final round.

When at last Setanta set out, he was a full mile behind them. Meanwhile, Culann greeted his guests with open arms. Before the feast

began, Culann raised his voice, 'My friends, I must ask: are all within? For I must release my hound to guard the house.'

This hound was no ordinary beast. He was vast, fierce as a lion, strong enough to be held only with three chains, each pulled by three men. None in Ulster dared trespass while Culann's hound stood guard.

'All are here!' cried the king, forgetting in his merriment the boy who lagged behind. So Culann loosed his hound.

The night was still when Setanta came over the hill. He had scarcely set foot near the smith's dwelling when the beast burst from the shadows. The hound's growls rumbled like thunder, its eyes blazing, its fangs bared to tear the intruder apart.

Setanta's heart quickened. He looked about for a weapon, but he carried nothing save his hurley and sliotar.

The hound leapt.

In that heartbeat, Setanta struck his sliotar with all his might. It flew like lightning, straight down the hound's throat. With a terrible yelp, the beast fell, the ball tearing through its body. The mighty guard dog lay still upon the earth, slain by a boy's hand.

At that moment, inside the hall, Conchobar started upright.

'We have forgotten Setanta!' he cried.

The company rushed out, fearing to find the boy in pieces. Instead, they beheld him standing, tall and calm, over the body of Culann's dread hound.

'By the gods,' whispered Conchobar, 'what a warrior this boy shall be.'

But Culann himself had come out and, seeing his hound, cried in grief:

'My hound! My faithful companion, my guard, my pride! Gone, gone forever!'

Setanta bowed his head in sorrow. 'Forgive me, master smith. Your hound would have slain me, and I had no choice. Yet it is a heavy thing to rob you of so loyal a companion.'

He paused, then lifted his eyes. 'I will make amends. Until you have raised another pup strong enough to guard your hall, I shall be your hound. I shall defend your house as faithfully as the beast you lost.'

The hall fell silent at his words.

At last, Culann spoke through his tears. 'So be it. No hound could guard my home better than the boy who felled this one.'

Conchobar laughed and placed a hand on his nephew's shoulder. 'Then all hail Cú Chulainn – the Hound of Culann!'

The knights raised the cry together: 'Cú Chulainn! Cú Chulainn!' Setanta smiled, for he found he liked the name well. And though he was still but a boy, from that night forward he bore the name by which he would be remembered forever: Cú Chulainn, greatest of Ulster's warriors, the Hound of Culann.

Setanta Becomes Cú Chulainn

The Coming of Lugh, God of Light

Long, long ago, before the time of Fionn and Cú Chulainn, there dwelt a divine race in Ireland known as the Tuatha Dé Danann. Some said they were ancient tribes steeped in magic, others said they were fallen angels who had found a home upon the emerald isle. Whatever their origin, there was no doubting their majesty. Their court at Tara shone with light even when storms darkened the skies. Their faces gleamed with a beauty so bright it hurt to look upon them, and their skill in crafts, magic, and song was greater than any known to mere mortals.

Yet though they were splendid, they lived under the shadow of tyranny. From the depths of the sea had risen a monstrous race, the Fomor, whose cruelty was without limit. They crushed the people of Ireland beneath their heel, pillaging villages, plundering treasure and sowing ruin wherever they passed. Their lord was the most dreadful of all: Balor of the Evil Eye.

Balor was a giant of hideous form. His frame was many times the size of a man, and in his forehead he bore an eye so terrible that none could endure its gaze. Kept closed beneath a heavy lid, the eye was opened only when Balor willed destruction. At a glance, armies fell dead, crops withered and fields turned to ash. From his glass tower on Tory Island, he watched Ireland with one eye, and when anger took him, he opened the other and dealt death across the land.

So the Fomor ruled, and none dared rise against them. But prophecy is a dangerous thing, and many years before, a seer had foretold that Balor would one day be slain — not by any rival, no warrior or king, but by his own grandson.

Balor raged when he heard it. He was Balor of the Mighty Blows, Balor of the Evil Eye — no one could kill him! Yet fear ate at him. He had but one daughter,

Ethlinn, and he swore she would never bear a child. To make certain, he locked her in a high stone tower upon Tory Island, guarded by twelve women who were tasked to never let her see the face of a man.

For years Ethlinn lived in that lonely tower, gazing out to sea. She knew nothing of men, save the shadows she glimpsed on the sails of ships far off upon the waves, and in her dreams she saw faces that filled her heart with longing. She begged her guards to tell her of the world beyond, but they would not answer. She was to live and die in solitude, never knowing love.

Balor, believing himself safe from the prophecy, grew greedy. His eye turned not only to conquest but to treasure. One day he heard tale of a wondrous cow, owned by Cian, one of three brothers of the Tuatha Dé Danann. This cow, the Glas Gaibhnenn, was unlike any beast of earth – her milk never failed, her hide shone like silk in the sun, and she was twice the size of other cattle. Balor desired her above all things. So one dark night he came with his monstrous followers, seized the cow, and carried her off to Tory Island.

When Cian discovered the theft, he burned with rage. His brothers warned him, 'Do not be foolish, no man can withstand the Evil Eye. To go after Balor is to march to death.' But Cian would not rest. He went to the wise druidess Birog, who dwelt upon a windswept mountain.

'Balor has stolen my cow,' Cian said. 'Tell me how I may reclaim her when no man can set foot on his cursed island.'

Birog studied him and replied, 'You speak truly – no man may reach that place. But a woman may.' Then with a cunning smile she disguised him in her own garments, braided his hair, and with her magic she called the wind. 'Twelve hours you have, before the breeze that bears you away brings you back. But beware – you may find more than cattle there.' With that she blew upon his brow, and Cian was lifted on the wind and carried across the sea to Tory Island.

There the guards of Ethlinn's tower were watchful and they surrounded Cian on the shore at once. 'Who comes to this forbidden isle?' they demanded.

'I am but a woman of the Tuatha Dé Danann,' Cian answered, 'fleeing hardship, seeking only refuge.'

The guards, taken by pity and respect for the divine race, let him within. That night, as silence fell and the women slept, Cian dispensed with his disguise and wandered through the tower. After an hour's search he cursed, 'My cow must be around here somewhere!' But then a sound met his ears so beautiful that all thought of his stolen cow vanished.

It was the voice of a woman and the melody carried him up the stairs like a siren. When he reached the topmost door he wandered through, entranced, in a dream. Ethlinn's singing faltered. She gazed at Cian astounded, 'I know you. You are the man in my dreams.'

'And you,' said Cian, 'are the woman of mine.'

So love took them that night, swift and fated. But as dawn broke, the wind rose again, and though Cian longed to stay, the spell carried him back across the sea, leaving Ethlinn alone once more. She did not know what had happened to Cian, but not long thereafter he was gone from the world.

Nine months passed. Ethlinn hid her sorrow from her terrible father but she could not hide her swelling belly. In time Cian's child was born to her – a boy with golden hair and light in his eyes. In a fury Balor sought Cian out and killed him without mercy. Next, he turned to the baby. Terrified of the prophecy, he commanded the infant to be cast into a whirlpool at sea.

But Ethlinn cried to the wind, 'Save him! His name is Lugh, and he is my son!' Her plea reached the ears of Birog, who swept down in a fury of magic and plucked the babe from the waves. She carried him away in secret, far from Balor's grasp, and raised him as her own.

Thus Lugh grew in hiding, fostered by the wise druidess. She taught him all she knew – to fight, to heal, to sing, to craft, to conjure. No matter the skill, Lugh mastered it, for a fire burned within him. Each time he faltered, the thought of Balor, murderer of his father and tyrant of Ireland, gave him strength.

He vowed he would become greater than any man, so that one day he might fulfil the prophecy.

Eighteen years passed. Then came the day when Nuada, King of the Tuatha Dé Danann, held a great feast at Tara. As the revelry echoed through the halls, a knock sounded at the gate. The doorkeeper, Gamal, opened it and found a young man standing tall, his eyes bright as stars.

'I am Lugh, son of Cian of the Tuatha Dé Danann, and of Ethlinn, daughter of Balor,' said the stranger. 'I seek audience with your king.'

Gamal frowned. 'Only those with great skill may enter this hall. What craft have you?'

'I am a carpenter.'

'We have one who shapes wood as though it were clay.'

'Then I am a smith.'

'Our smith bends steel harder than a dragon's scale.'

'Then I am a champion.'

'Our champion is stronger than any man alive.'

'I am a harper, a poet, a magician.'

'We have harpers who could make you weep, poets who would make you question your soul, magicians who could unmake reality.'

'Then let me be your cup-bearer.'

'We have nine already,' Gamal snapped.

But then Lugh said, 'Ask your king if he has one man who can do all these things together. If he does, I shall leave at once and never return.'

Gamal carried the challenge to King Nuada, who laughed aloud. 'If such a man exists, he may take my throne itself! Bring him in!'

So Lugh entered the hall, and before the assembled company he displayed his gifts. He plucked the harp and played music more moving than any heard before. He recited verse so rich that warriors wept. He conjured illusions that left all gasping. He crafted a perfect cup, forged a shining blade from rusted iron, and with it defeated the king's own champion in single combat.

A hush fell, broken only when Nuada rose. 'Truly you are master of all arts. Take my throne for six days, a day for each gift you have shown.'

But Lugh shook his head. 'I need but one day. On that day, I ask that the Tuatha Dé Danann march with me against the Fomor.'

A murmur ran through the hall. For long had the gods and people suffered Balor's oppression. Now Lugh stood before them, shining with destiny, and their hearts stirred. They raised their voices in a great cry of assent.

So Lugh set about raising an army. For a year the Tuatha Dé Danann forged weapons, sharpened spears, hammered armour and trained. Across Ireland men flocked to Lugh's banner, encouraged by his words and the fire of hope he carried.

At last, on the appointed day, Lugh returned to Tara at the head of a vast host. The sun blazed upon spearheads and banners, and the gods themselves seemed to stride with him.

'My people!' cried Lugh. 'Too long have we cowered beneath Balor's eye. Too long have we been broken and robbed. Today we rise, and Ireland shall be free!' With that the Tuatha Dé Danann marched to war.

Upon the plain of Mag Tuired the two hosts met. The Fomor came in countless number, towering and monstrous. Their roars shook the earth,

The Coming of Lugh, God of Light

their weapons gleamed with ruin. Against them the Tuatha Dé Danann charged with battle cries, the earth trembling beneath their feet.

The clash was like thunder. Blades rang, shields splintered, cries of pain and fury filled the air. The Tuatha Dé Danann fought with the fury of lions, yet the Fomor pressed them hard. Then into the battle strode Balor himself, his monstrous form blotting the sun. With a dreadful cry he opened his terrible eye. Death swept across the field. Warriors dropped like grain before the scythe. Fear spread, and the Tuatha Dé Danann faltered.

But Lugh stood firm. He did not look upon the eye, but instead he fitted a stone into his sling. With steady hand he took aim. The stone whistled through the air and struck Balor square in the forehead.

Balor howled, his mighty head reeling back. His

evil eye rolled into his skull, its deadly gaze falling upon his own people. Hundreds of Fomor shrieked and died beneath its blast. Then Balor staggered, toppled and fell to the earth with a crash like a mountain splitting. And thus the prophecy was fulfilled – slain by his own grandson, Balor of the Evil Eye was no more.

The Fomor fled, their power broken, and the plain rang with the cheers of the Tuatha Dé Danann. They lifted Lugh high upon their shoulders, hailing him as saviour. King Nuada himself removed his crown and knelt before him.

'The day belongs to Lugh,' he declared. 'Without him we would all be lost. He is our true king.'

So it was that Lugh, God of Light, took the throne of the Tuatha Dé Danann, and under his rule the land flourished once more.

The Death of Cú Chulainn

After years of heroism, adventure and battles, the stories of Cú Chulainn were sung far and wide across Ireland. He was swift as the wind, strong as an ox, as powerful as a god – some feared him but to most he was beloved. For he stood for honour, duty and protection of his people. But fate comes for the good as surely as it come for the bad.

Years earlier Cú Chulainn had spurned the Morrígan, the phantom queen of battle. She had sought his love but his life was bound to the people, not a god. For this insult she cursed him. Atop a mountain in the Otherworld, the goddess screamed, 'Cú Chulainn shall die at the height of his youth, at the peak of his strength, in the full bloom of his glory!'

Druids read the prophecy in dark omens and the word swept the land. Cú Chulainn knew well his fate. Though he had never sought to escape it, only to meet it standing.

The Death of Cú Chulainn

Years had passed since the Táin Bó Cúailnge, the great cattle raid of Cooley, when Maeve of Connacht had led her armies against Ulster and been held at bay by the boy hero Cú Chulainn. Now Maeve thirsted once more for vengeance. During the battle Cú Chulainn had slain Calatin the great sorcerer. Maeve called upon his 26 sons and countless grandsons and promised them their revenge. Dripping in dark magic, poison and curses, they descended from the west. Leaving a trail of destruction in their wake, the terrible band drove forward in search of the Ulsterman.

Thus was the snare laid, and the hounds of doom set loose.

On the last morning of his life, Cú Chulainn's wife Emer pleaded with him, 'My love, please do not go. You have won every battle you have ever fought but today the omens are dire. There is silence outside save for the ravens' caw. They are the harbingers of death. And above all my heart warns me. Stay.'

Emer clutched at her husband's sleeve, 'Emer, I cannot sit here while the people of Ulster suffer. I would not be your husband if I did so. If I must die, let it be standing, sword in hand.'

And so Cú Chulainn rode forth from Eamhain Macha, his chariot wheels singing on the stones, driven by his loyal charioteer Láeg. His horses, Liath Macha and Dub Sainglend, screamed as though they sensed the end drawing near. Ravens circled overhead.

Like all heroes of the old world, Cú Chulainn lived under *geasa* – a magical vow. To break them was to unravel the thread of one's life. His enemies knew this, and so they schemed.

At a crossroads, an old woman bent by age sat roasting dog's flesh upon a spit. She beckoned him.

'Great Cú Chulainn,' she croaked. 'It would honour me to share my meal with a hero such as you.'

But one of his *geasa* forbade him from ever eating the flesh of a dog, for he had taken the name of the hound as his own. To eat it was to eat of himself. Yet another *geis* bound him never to refuse hospitality. He could not obey both.

With grim heart he sat, took the meat and ate. At once his strength withered. His knees trembled beneath him. The Morrígan had taken her payment, and the path to death yawned wide.

Not long after, messengers came in haste. The armies of Connacht were upon Ulster again, led by the sons of Calatin thirsty for revenge.

Cú Chulainn armed himself. His weapons shone like fire in the morning sun, and a battle frenzy burned in his eyes. Though weakened, he would not sit idle while enemies trampled his land.

On the plain of Muirthemne he wheeled his chariot against the hoard, one against hundreds. Again and again he charged, and the fury of the Hound of Ulster was like a storm. Warriors fell like rain upon him. Swords clashed against his amour, arrows pierced his shield, but none could strike him down.

Yet fate crept ever nearer.

The sons of Calatin unleashed their final, dreadful weapon – four spears upon which they had placed wicked magic, an old dark spell for a weapon to always find its mark.

The first throw struck Láeg, the faithful charioteer, and he fell lifeless beside the horses he loved.

The second pierced Dub Sainglend, the dark horse, and it crashed in death upon the plain.

The third struck Liath Macha, the grey of Macha, who screamed like a man as he died, blood foaming from his nostrils.

And the fourth – the deadliest of

all – found Cú Chulainn. It pierced his side, and his blood poured out like a river. The hero staggered, but still he did not fall.

Knowing the end had come, Cú Chulainn refused to give his enemies the sight of him lying in the dirt. Wounded unto death, he dragged himself to a great standing stone that jutted from the plain. With his own bloodied hands, he lashed himself upright to it. Cú Chulainn cried out to the evil rabble, 'Come then! I am still strong enough to fight you all and even if you strike me I shall never fall!'

There he stood, dying on his feet, sword in hand, shield upon his arm, facing the westering sun. His enemies gathered at a distance but dared not come near, for the hero's eyes still blazed with the light of battle. Even bleeding, even broken, he looked as though he might strike again at any moment.

Hour after hour they watched. The sky reddened. Still he stood. None dared approach.

At last a black shape descended from the sky. A raven, sleek and terrible, landed upon Cú Chulainn's shoulder and pecked at the blood upon him. It was the Morrígan, the crow of battle, come to claim her due.

Only then did the warriors know he was truly dead. They crept forward like jackals, and one cut off his head to bear as a trophy to Maeve.

His body they left tied to the stone, but no man who looked upon it ever forgot.

When word reached Ulster, a cry of mourning rose that shook the hills. Deirdre had been the sorrow of Ulster, but Cú Chulainn was its glory, and now that glory was gone.

Some say his father, the god Lugh, descended in a blaze of light and struck down those who had defiled his son. Others say that the land itself wept, rivers swelling with grief, trees bowing their heads.

But whether by godly vengeance or mortal memory, one truth remained: the Hound of Ulster, though slain, had won immortality. For his name was sung by every poet, told by every bard and carried through the ages until even now, when his deeds are spoken beside those of Achilles or Heracles.

He had stood alone. He had met death on his feet. He had burned brighter than any flame, though flames burn short.

Thus ends the tale of Cú Chulainn, the mightiest warrior of Ireland, whose death was his crowning glory.

The Death of Cú Chulainn

The King with the Donkey Ears

Long after the time the vain and capricious gods ruled over Ireland, there ruled a man who made them seem almost humble. His name was King Labhraidh Loingseach, and a fearsome king he was. Ruthless, stern and swift in judgement, no other lord dared rise against him. He was powerful beyond measure, with lands stretching wider than a man could ride in a day, castles bedecked with banners, and treasure halls brimming with gold, silver and jewels. He had all a man could ever desire but he also had a secret.

Beneath his shining crown, hidden beneath a careful fall of golden hair, King Labhraidh bore a pair of donkey's ears. Long, grey and furry they were, twitching like those of an ass. He had been born with them and no matter the land he gained, the gold he made or the castles he built, nothing could assuage his shame. But even greater than his shame was his

The King with the Donkey Ears

fear that one day someone would find out.

To hide the ears, he kept his hair long and carefully arranged. But once each year a dreadful time came when he simply had to have a haircut. Since no man could be trusted with such a secret, the king put every barber who touched his hair to death.

Year after year, the king's messengers would fetch some poor barber from the countryside, and though the man would enter the castle alive, he never left. At first people whispered, then they noticed. Soon the barbers of Ireland grew few, and the people's hair grew wild and tangled, for none dared risk the king's summons. Mothers wept for sons, wives for husbands, children for fathers – all lost to the secret shame of their ruler.

Yet fate always finds its way. In Labhraidh's kingdom there lived a young man named Dónal, the only son of a widowed mother. Dónal had a gift with scissors – he could cut and shape hair so finely that even the proudest lady or the sternest warrior left his chair smiling. To him, barbering was not a trade but an art, and he dreamed of becoming the most skilled barber in all of Ireland.

His poor mother lived in terror.

'Ah, Dónal,' she would say, wringing her hands, 'why could you not be a farmer, or a knight, or even a wandering harper? Anything would be safer! What if the king's messenger comes for you? You'll never be seen again.'

Dónal only laughed. He was young and brilliant and without a care in the world.

'Mother,' said he, 'you believe too much in old wives' tales. Perhaps those barbers angered the king by giving him poor cuts. But I – I am the best barber in the land. If I lay my hands upon the king's head, he'll be so pleased he'll shower us with gold.'

As though the gods were listening, there came a knock upon the door.

Dónal's mother froze. She peered through the small window and gave a cry, clutching her son. 'It is the king's messenger! Hide, hide, my boy!'

But Dónal merely shook back his glorious hair and opened the door.

'I come on behalf of King Labhraidh Loingseach,' said the messenger in a voice as sharp as steel. 'Your son is summoned to the castle. The king has chosen him for a task of great honour.'

The mother wailed, clutching Dónal's arm. 'Please, don't take him! He is all I have in this world.'

But Dónal gently pried her hands free. 'I must go, Mother. It is the king's command.'

And so, though his heart ached to leave her, Dónal followed the messenger. But his mother would not surrender so easily. She leapt upon her horse and rode hard for the castle, burst into the hall and threw herself at the king's feet.

'Mercy, o king!' she cried. 'My son is my only comfort in my old age. Spare his life, I beg you, as you would wish your own mother to be spared her grief.'

Now, King Labhraidh was not a gentle man. His will was iron, and his wrath swift. Yet something in the woman's plea stirred his heart, for she reminded him of his own mother, long buried.

He frowned, thought deeply, and at last declared: 'Your son may live, but only on one condition. He must swear never to speak of what he sees in this castle. If his lips remain sealed, his life will be spared.'

The next day, Dónal was brought into the king's private chamber. No guards remained, no servants – only the king himself, grim and watchful.

'I have spoken with your mother,' said Labhraidh. 'You must swear to me now: whatever you see here, you shall tell no living soul.'

'I swear it, my king,' said Dónal, his heart pounding.

'Promise?' growled the king.

'I promise,' whispered the barber.

Then, with slow hands, King Labhraidh lifted his crown. He shook out his long hair, and there – revealed at last – stood the donkey's ears.

Dónal's eyes widened, and a gasp leapt from his throat before he could stop it.

The king's gaze darkened.

But Dónal, quick with his scissors, bent to his work. Carefully, skilfully, he trimmed the royal locks, shaping them so that the ears were hidden once more. He dared not speak, dared not even breathe

too loudly, and when the task was finished, he bowed low and fled from the chamber.

All the way home he kept his lips sealed tight, not answering a word to any who hailed him.

At first his mother rejoiced to see him alive. 'Dónal! My darling boy, you are safe!' she cried, hugging him close. But she soon saw the shadow in his eyes. He hardly spoke, ate less and he cut no hair save when forced. He grew pale and thin, as though some poison were festering inside him.

At last, desperate, his mother brought him to a druid, wise in the ways of men's hearts.

The druid looked upon Dónal and shook his head.

'The boy holds a secret too heavy for his

spirit. He must let it out, or it will consume him.'

'But he cannot!' cried the mother. 'He swore never to speak of what he saw, not to any living soul.'

The druid closed his eyes, meditated long, and then smiled.

'There is a way. Let him go into the forest, and whisper the secret to a tree. A tree is no living person, and so his oath will remain unbroken. The burden will leave him, and peace return.'

So Dónal did as the druid said. He walked deep into the woods until he found a great willow tree by a singing stream. Its branches drooped low, trailing in the water, and its leaves whispered like voices in the wind.

Dónal pressed his lips close to the swaying leaves and whispered: 'The king has donkey's ears.'

He whispered it again and again, until at last the weight lifted from his heart. His shoulders straightened, his colour returned, and for the first time in many months, he smiled.

But fate is never simple.

Not long after, a harper from the king's court came wandering through the forest. His old harp had broken, and he sought wood to fashion a new one. When he saw the great willow by the stream, he knew its wood would resonate more sweetly than any other.

He cut a branch, shaped it into a harp and strung it with care. That very night, he brought it to the king's hall, where nobles and commoners alike gathered for a feast.

'Play!' cried King Labhraidh, eager for music.

The harper set his fingers to the strings and a most strange thing happened. The harp began to sing on its own, as though the very wood had a voice. And what it sang was this:

> *The king, the king, has donkey's ears,*
> *A secret carried through long years.*
> *The king, the king, let all men know,*
> *From the crown of his head the grey ears grow.*

The hall fell silent. The king leapt to his feet, his face red with fury. He seized at the harp, but in the struggle his crown flew from his head. And there, for all to see, were the donkey ears in their full, twitching length.

For a long heartbeat, there was silence. Then one child giggled. A woman laughed. Soon the hall rang with laughter from high lords to low servants.

The king froze. He looked about him, expecting mockery, hatred, scorn. But what he saw was only mirth – warm, harmless mirth.

One of the chiefs spoke: 'My lord, it is nothing. You are still our king. What are donkey's ears to us, when your hand is strong and your will unbroken?'

The harper bowed. 'No one cares, my lord. The secret was heavier on you than on us.'

And slowly, King Labhraidh began to laugh as well. He laughed at himself, at the long years of fear, at the foolishness of trying to hide what could not be hidden forever.

From that day on, he no longer slew his barbers. He no longer troubled to hide his ears. And strangely enough, he was a better, happier king for it. The land prospered and the people rejoiced, especially the barbers who could now practice their art without fear.

The King with the Donkey Ears

The Birth of Fionn

Long ago in the misty hills of Éire there lived a man called Cumhal Mac Art. Many great deeds were attached to the name and always it was spoken in reverence. He was the greatest champion west of Erin, a warrior and leader of the Fianna. He knew that he was admired, even adored, but he envied normal people far more than they him. For he was fated to walk the world alone. Many years before a druid had made a dire prophecy to him, 'Do not ever marry, Cumhal Mac Art, for if you do death will find you the very next day.'

From that day forward Cumhal steeled his heart. He poured his energies into duty, battle and adventure. He gained power, fame and fortune but he would have given it all in a heartbeat for love.

But Cumhal rejected the advances of every young woman who pursued him. These were many and frequent, for besides being leader of the

Fianna, he was most handsome. Whenever they spoke to him, eyes fluttering, he kept his firmly to the ground. For fifteen long years he shut away his heart. He felt almost dead inside like an empty shell, washed and buffeted along the shore. Madness crept close. His life seeped into a strange dreamlike quality until something happened that made reality clang like a bell.

One windswept day he was riding past a grand castle when he saw a princess staring out of a window. Cumhal gasped. Her hair gleamed like a river of dark gold, her eyes were deep as twilight and a beautiful melancholy played about her brow. She was nothing less than the most heart-stopping woman Cumhal had ever seen, 'Fair maiden, why do you dream so?' He said, in spite of himself.

'Because I am imprisoned, good sir. My father, the king, has locked me in this tower. I am doomed to dream alone.'

'Why would a father do such a cruel thing …

I'm sorry I don't know your name?'

The woman smiled, making Cumhal blush. 'They call me Muirne.' The melancholy crossed her face once more, 'My father believes that if I ever marry and have a baby, the baby will grow up to take his throne. It was a prophecy foretold.'

At those words, Cumhal felt the sting of his own fate press upon him. He knew the danger of prophecy. He knew the cost. Yet, even as his heart whispered caution, his spirit burned with love for the maiden he had only just met.

Day after day he returned to the tower, speaking to her from below, carrying little gifts, and telling jokes to lighten her sorrow. Soon, their words turned tender, and then they turned into vows. At last, unable to resist, Cumhal carried a priest up the narrow winding stairs, and there, in the secrecy of her prison chamber, he and Muirne married.

But fate had not forgotten its promise. The very next

dawn, the war horns of the Fianna sounded

across the land. Drums thundered; enemies had come to raid. Cumhal, though he feared what would come, strapped on his armor and went to his mother, Liath Luachra.

'Mother,' he said urgently, 'I have taken a wife. And now there is a prophecy bound to her also. Should she bear a child, my enemies will seek his life. If the child is born, you must protect him.'

Liath laid her hands on her son's shoulders. 'Then go to battle with no fear, my child. If the gods grant you a son, I will keep him safe from every danger.'

Cumhal embraced her tightly. 'Remember, Mother – watch for him, guard him well.'

And with that, he rode off for battle. Like every warrior before him, Cumhal hoped he might be the one to slip past destiny's snare. But prophecy is a net from which no man wriggles free. In the clash of shields and the roar of war cries, Cumhal fell, his blood darkening the earth by sunset.

Nine months passed. Muirne wept for her lost husband, yet within her womb she carried his legacy. At last, she bore a son, a boy with hair as white as snow, as though moonlight itself had taken the form of a child. She named him Fionn, meaning 'fair' or 'bright'.

She tried to hide him from her father, the king. She dressed in plain garments, hid in her chambers and muffled every cry of labour. But no woman can silence the wail of a newborn. The king, hearing the cries, stormed into her room in a fury.

'So it is true!' he bellowed. 'The cursed child is born!'

Before Muirne could plead, the king snatched the infant from her arms and hurled him from the tower window.

But Liath, faithful to her vow, had been watching below. Swift as a hawk, she leapt and caught the babe before he touched the ground. Clutching him to her breast, she fled into the shadowed forest, the king's guards crying out behind her.

The king's rage was boundless. He swore that no white-haired child would live within his kingdom. From that day, he ordered his men to kill any child unlucky enough to be born with blonde hair.

Yet Liath was cunning and fierce. She carried Fionn deep into the heart of the forest, to a place where the trees grew so thick the sun's rays barely touched the moss. There she paid a woodsman to hollow out a mighty oak, crafting for them a secret dwelling. In this dark shelter, she raised Fionn in silence and secrecy.

Years passed, and Fionn grew strong. Liath trained him as she had once trained his father – teaching him to run with the swiftness of a deer, to fight with strength beyond his years, and to play hurling with unmatched skill. His eyes were keen as an eagle's, sharpened by years of twilight in the oak's shade.

One day, Liath judged it time to test him. She brought him to the Tailteann Games, where warriors gathered for contests of skill. A great hurling match was underway between the king's men and the champions of Ulster.

As Fionn stepped into the light

of the field, the crowd gasped. His hair, pale and gleaming, marked him at once.

'There! Seize him!' the king's men shouted.

Panic rippled. Liath grasped Fionn's hand and ran, but the soldiers gave chase. Through woods they fled until they reached a bog. Liath slowed; she knew she was hindering him.

'Run, Fionn!' she cried. 'Do not look back!'

And with a fierce cry, she threw herself into the bog, sinking beneath the mire until only her hair floated on the surface.

When the soldiers arrived, they saw the pale hair glistening and believed Fionn had drowned. They cut a lock as proof and carried it to the king, who rejoiced. He could breathe freely once more.

The Birth of Fionn

But Fionn lived on, hidden by the sacrifice of his grandmother. Alone now, he wept bitterly in a cave, the walls echoing his sorrow. Yet as grief hollowed him, a new strength filled him. 'She died for me,' he whispered. 'I must live to honour her.'

To disguise himself, he cut his hair short and stained it dark with crushed roots and leaves.

He ventured forth into the wide world.

Not long after, he came upon men labouring in a clearing. They were builders, stacking timber for a castle. Fionn approached curiously.

'What are you building?' he asked.

'A fortress for the king,' one worker grumbled. 'But every night, some wretch

sets it aflame, and by dawn we are left with ashes. The king has sworn to give his daughter's hand to any man who can stop it.'

Fionn grinned. 'Then perhaps this is a task for me.'

The men warned him: 'Many have tried. Those who fail are cast into the king's dungeons.'

But Fionn was undaunted. That night, he hid among the trees. His eyes, sharpened by years of shadow, pierced the darkness. Around midnight, he spied a cloaked figure creeping toward the new-built castle. With a torch the figure set it ablaze, then fled into the forest.

Silent as a cat, Fionn followed, leaping from branch to branch. At last, the figure reached a cottage. Fionn dropped down upon him, and they wrestled until Fionn pinned him fast.

'Who are you?' Fionn demanded.

'I am the woodsman's son,' the boy spat.

'Why burn the king's castle?'

'Because it is our land! He steals our forest. Every stone he lays is an insult to my father.'

The Birth of Fionn

Fionn frowned, thinking quickly. 'But each time you burn it, he cuts down more of your forest to rebuild. You harm yourself more than him.'

The boy hesitated, realising the truth.

'Swear to me,' Fionn said firmly, 'you will stop, or I will tell the king and bring his wrath upon this house.'

Reluctantly, the boy agreed.

The next morning, Fionn strode boldly into the king's hall.

'You?' sneered the king. 'What brings a mucky youth like you here?'

'I have solved your mystery,' Fionn declared. 'Your castle will stand.'

The king laughed harshly. 'If you succeed, boy, you may have my daughter's hand.'

Fionn's eyes burned. 'I want not your daughter – I want your kingdom.'

The hall erupted in laughter, but the king, amused, agreed. 'Very well! If you save my castle, the crown shall be yours.'

That night, as promised, no fire came. At dawn, the castle stood untouched.

The king raged but could not deny his oath. Reluctantly, he yielded the throne to Fionn. The boy's first act was to free the prisoners from the dungeons, including his own mother from her tower.

Muirne embraced him, weeping with joy. 'Three cheers for my son, Fionn mac Cumhaill!' she cried.

And so the people cheered, and the legend of Fionn began. From that day, he gathered champions around him. The Fianna was reborn, stronger than ever. And though his path was long and filled with peril, his story was only beginning.

The Birth of Fionn

The Giant's Causeway

Fionn mac Cumhaill had reached manhood. He lived with his wife, Una, in a strong stone house on the cliffs of Antrim. The waves pounded endlessly against the black rocks below, and the gulls wheeled overhead.

He had built the stone house himself. Fishermen marvelled as he hurled boulders up the cliffs. He was said to have the strength of five hundred men. He could tear up trees by their roots but he could also leap across valleys and his voice could travel so far that shepherds on distant hills mistook it for thunder. He was greatly feared by his enemies but loved by his people. He was the guardian of the Emerald Isle, the leader of the Fianna and the greatest of all warriors. The stories of him were sung far and wide – in taverns, in castles, in villages, in ships sailing

far across the sea. Everyone knew the name Fionn mac Cumhaill and in people's minds he was giant. However, as large as Fionn was — truly twice the size of a normal man — he was still a man.

But across the sea, in Scotland, there lived a true giant — one whose name struck terror into every mouth that dared to speak it: Benandonner.

Benandonner was colossal. Taller than the tallest oak, with arms like pillars and hands that could shatter stone. His roar caused landslides, and his feet crushed forests. The people of Scotland lived in terror and only ever spoke of him in a whisper. But most unfortunately, people went as far as to sing about the great Fionn mac Cumhaill. Benandonner heard and the tales drove him into a fury. He heard how brave Fionn was, how ferocious, how very giant he was. Jealousy flamed in Benandonner. None could be greater than him. He would challenge this puny pretender and pound him into a pulp. Afterwards there would be no question as to who was the greatest, most terrifying giant in all the world.

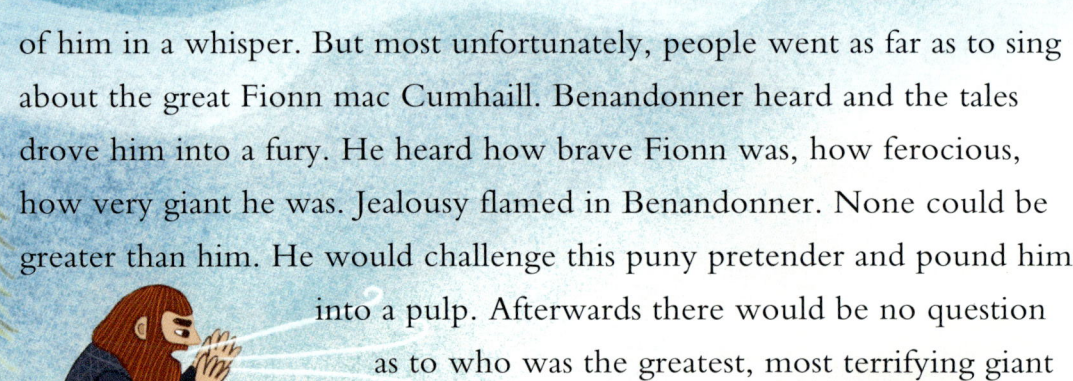

One stormy morning, Benandonner climbed to the cliffs of Staffa, the winds whipping his cloak, and stared across the sea to Ireland. He filled his massive lungs until the birds scattered in terror, and his voice rolled out like thunder.

'Fionn mac Cumhaill!' he bellowed, the

very waves recoiling from his roar.

'I am Benandonner, the greatest of all giants! I challenge you in a fight to the death! Refuse and all of Scotland and Ireland shall know you for a coward!'

Fionn was sitting at his hearth in Antrim, enjoying a quiet meal with Una when he heard the terrible sound. People said his voice carried far but it was nothing compared to the thunderous rumble that challenged him. At first he thought it was thunder, then the moaning of the wind – but soon he caught his own name echoing within it.

Startled, he leapt to his feet, knocking the table sideways, and rushed down to the shore. Standing on the black rocks, he heard the words clearly:

'Fight me, or be shamed forever!'

Fionn's blood boiled. So some giant from across the sea dared to challenge him. He had slain monster and dragons, held back entire armies by himself. He had never turned from a challenge in his life and he wasn't planning to start today. Fionn cupped his great hands around his mouth and roared back with all his might:

'Benandonner! I hear you, and I accept! Stay where you are, and I'll come across to you at once!'

With that, Fionn set to work. He tore great basalt stones from the shore and hurled them into the sea, one after another. Each rock fell with a crash, sending up white sprays of foam. Slowly, step-by-step, a strange path began to stretch across the waves: hexagonal and octagonal pillars, rising like black teeth from the water.

The tide fought him, the sea trying to swallow the stones, but Fionn was relentless. Sweat ran down his brow as he built his path, each rock a stepping-stone toward Scotland.

Hours passed. At last, exhausted but determined, Fionn set foot on the Isle of Staffa.

There, he found Benandonner and froze. Most fortunately, the giant seemed to have tired himself out with all the bellowing and had fallen asleep right on the shore.

Fionn crept closer. Even in slumber, the Scottish giant was terrifying. His chest rose and fell like a living hill. Each breath rattled the stones around him. His hands were like slabs of rock, and his teeth were as big as paving stones.

Fionn's courage faltered. He had thought himself a giant, but next to Benandonner he seemed hardly more than a child.

'Gods save us,' he muttered. 'He's three times my size … his hands alone could squash me like an apple.'

Panic took him. Quiet as a fox, Fionn turned and fled back across the causeway, his heart hammering louder than the sea.

Bursting through the door of his house, Fionn was pale and trembling. Una looked up from her spinning.

'Husband? What's the matter? You're white as milk.'

Fionn tried to compose himself but failed.

'Una … I may have … accepted a challenge.'

Her eyes narrowed.

'From whom?'

'Benandonner,' Fionn admitted. 'He's coming, Una. He's vast … larger than I ever imagined. I thought myself strong, but beside him I am a mere boy.'

Una's knitting needles faltered. She stared at her husband.

'So, you cannot beat him with strength.'

Fionn sank into a chair, despairing.

'He'll cross the causeway soon. He'll smash our house to pieces. He'll grind me into dust.'

Una's brow furrowed. She was clever, far cleverer than most gave her credit for. At last she stood, eyes flashing with sudden inspiration.

'Then we won't fight him with strength. We'll fight him with cunning.'

She rushed to her basket and pulled out a great ball of wool. Her needles flew.

'Una!' Fionn cried. 'You're knitting? At a time like this?'

'This is the plan, you great oaf. Do as I say – go outside and build a cradle. A huge one. Big enough for yourself.'

Still baffled, Fionn obeyed. In the yard, he cobbled together a vast cradle from planks and beams. By the time he dragged it inside, the ground was already trembling with approaching footsteps.

'Quick!' Una said. 'Put this on.'

She thrust into his hands the largest garments he had ever seen: a knitted bonnet, gown and booties.

'You want me to dress like a –'

'Like a baby,' Una snapped. 'Now hush, he's nearly here!'

Fionn swallowed his pride, donned the ridiculous outfit, and climbed into the cradle. He pulled the bonnet low to cover his beard.

A moment later, the door shook with earth-shattering blows.

'Fionn mac Cumhaill!' bellowed Benandonner. 'Come out and face me!'

Una, calm as still water, opened the window. 'Greetings great Benandonner. I was told to expect you today!' Benandonner's enormous head loomed before her.

'Where is he? Where is the Irish cur who dared challenge me?'

Una folded her arms.

'Fionn? Oh, he's away hunting in Derry just now. But you've come such a long way … why not step inside and rest? Only … hush your voice. You'll wake the baby.'

Benandonner blinked.

'The … baby?'

Una smiled sweetly and pointed to the cradle. There lay Fionn, bonnet pulled down, pretending to sleep.

The Scottish giant's jaw dropped. The baby was enormous – bigger than most men. If the child was so huge, what size must the father be?

Fear struck Benandonner's heart. He staggered back from the window, muttering.

'If that's the child … then the father … Gods above!'

Panic seized him. He turned and ran for his life. Across the causeway he thundered, his feet shaking the stones.

But even as he fled, a terrible thought struck him: What if Fionn follows me?

In his terror, Benandonner ripped up the stones of the causeway behind him, hurling them into the sea. By the time he reached Scotland, the path was broken, shattered, nothing but a trail of black stumps jutting from the waves.

And so it remains to this day. The mighty columns of basalt, hexagonal and perfect, stand on both the Antrim coast and the Isle of Staffa, but the path between is long gone.

When the thunder of Benandonner's retreat had faded, Fionn leapt from the cradle, tearing off the bonnet.

'Una! You genius of a woman!' he cried, crushing her in a grateful embrace. 'You saved me!'

Una laughed.

'Saved you? I saved Ireland, husband. Now perhaps next time you'll think before bellowing across the sea at giants!'

The Giant's Causeway

Diarmuid and Gráinne

Long ago, when Ireland was still a land of heroes, the Fianna roamed the forests and mountains. They were hunters, poets, warriors and, most importantly, guardians of the land. Among them was one man whose name was spoken with awe: Diarmuid Ó Duibhne. He was strong, swift and loyal, the right hand of Fionn mac Cumhaill himself. Yet his fame was not for strength alone. On his forehead was a mark, the Bol Sherca – the Love Spot. Whoever looked upon it was struck at once with irresistible love for him. To spare others and himself, Diarmuid wore his hair long and low, so that the spot remained hidden. For as sweet as love can be, it can turn sour in an instant.

Fionn was still the mightiest warrior in Ireland, though the years had begun to weigh on him. He had lost his wife many winters before.

Though he still hunted and feasted, though the Fianna's laughter filled his hall, he felt the ache of loneliness.

One night, with fire crackling in the great hearth, he spoke to his companions.

'My wife once told me that should she die she would not want me to spend the rest of my days alone. I have mourned long, so long she is becoming a dream.' He shook himself and let out a bark of laughter, 'You are all good company but it is time I took another wife! Tell me, who in all Ireland would be worthy?'

The warriors looked at one another.

'There is but one,' they said, 'Gráinne, daughter of High King Cormac mac Airt. None in Ireland is more virtuous, kind and beautiful.'

Fionn stroked his beard. He was old enough to be her

father, yet the match was fitting: the greatest leader with the High King's daughter. Too shy to speak his suit himself, he sent two ambassadors to King Cormac.

Now Gráinne had turned down many suitors. They brought her gold, jewels, silks – gifts from far and wide – but she had refused them all. For ever since she was twelve, her heart had belonged to one boy.

One stormy afternoon, she had stood by a window watching young warriors play hurling. Rain lashed, then sun broke through, and one boy's hair blew back in the wind. In that instant, her heart had been captured for life.

She had never forgotten him. That boy was Diarmuid Ó Duibhne.

So when Fionn's ambassadors came, her first thought was to refuse. But she hesitated.

The boy is gone, she thought. I have not seen him in years. Perhaps I never will. Fionn is noble, the greatest in Ireland. Perhaps I must wed him.

With a sigh, she agreed. Her father was delighted. He called a great feast to celebrate.

When the night came, the hall blazed with torches. The air was thick with music and the smell of roasted boar. Before she entered, Gráinne lingered behind a curtain, eager to see Fionn.

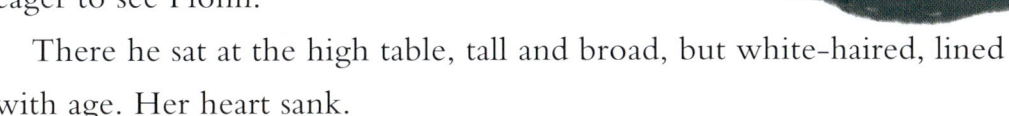

There he sat at the high table, tall and broad, but white-haired, lined with age. Her heart sank.

Then she saw the man beside him and gasped. It was the same boy from the hurling field, now grown into the most handsome warrior in Ireland – Diarmuid Ó Duibhne.

Her heart pounded. She could not marry Fionn. Her soul burned for Diarmuid. At once she hatched a plan.

She entered carrying a goblet of wine laced with a sleeping draught. Bowing low, she offered it to Fionn.

'My husband-to-be,' she said softly, 'drink, for this is the finest wine in the land.'

Fionn smiled, charmed by her beauty, and drank deep. His eyes closed, and he slumped in sleep. The feast was raucous around them, filled with cheer and drink and song, no one gave the sleeping Fionn a glance.

Gráinne turned to Diarmuid. Her voice trembled with passion.

'Warrior, I have loved you since I was a girl. Leave with me tonight. Be mine.'

Diarmuid's heart leapt at her beauty, yet dread filled him.

'My lady, I cannot,' he said. 'Fionn is my captain, my foster-father. To betray him is unthinkable.'

But Gráinne would not be denied. She raised her hand and spoke solemnly: 'You must flee with me. You cannot refuse. I place you under *geasa*.'

Fionn's son Oisín caught the last word and leaned forward, spilling wine, 'True, true, Diarmuid! No warrior may refuse a *geasa*, least of all one from the High King's daughter.'

Diarmuid's face darkened. He looked from Oisín to Gráinne.

'My heart is torn,' he whispered. 'But if this is your will, then I must obey.'

And so he rose and followed her into the night, grief already heavy in his chest.

Gráinne had dreamed of romance, but she was unaccustomed to hard travel. Soon her feet ached, her breath failed.

'Carry me,' she begged.

Diarmuid shook his head. 'If you tire, return to Fionn. This road is bitter.'

Just then, a light shone upon the path. Before them stood Aengus Óg, god of love.

'Two weary travellers I see,' he said. 'But your path is chosen. Here – take these horses.'

Two steeds appeared. Aengus laid his hand upon Diarmuid's shoulder.

'Beware. Fionn will soon wake. Hear my counsel: never sleep in a cave with one opening, nor in a house with one door. Never cook where you eat, nor sleep where you cook. Always keep moving. The road is your ally.' With that, he vanished.

Back at the feast, Fionn stirred. When he learned what had happened, his roar shook the rafters.

'Diarmuid – traitor! Men, saddle the horses. We ride!'

The Fianna thundered into pursuit.

Diarmuid and Gráinne fled across Ireland. From mountains to valleys, through forests and bogs, they travelled without rest.

For a year they evaded capture. Yet always the Fianna drew closer, finding traces: the ash of a fire, the bones of a fish, a remains of a camp.

At last, the couple found a house with seven doors. Believing themselves safe, they slept soundly.

But the Fianna surrounded the house, a warrior at each door.

Aengus Óg appeared again, shaking Diarmuid awake.

'You are trapped. The Fianna are at every door. Come, let me spirit you away.'

Diarmuid turned to Gráinne.

'Go with Aengus. He can save you. I must stay, and beg Fionn's forgiveness.'

'No!' she cried. 'I will not leave you.'

'Go!' Diarmuid commanded. His eyes were resolute.

Aengus drew Gráinne into his arms, and in a flash of light she was gone.

Diarmuid opened the first door and a grim warrior blocked his path. He tried the second, the third, the fourth – each guarded. At the seventh stood Fionn himself, rage burning in his eyes.

The Fianna closed in. But Diarmuid, nimble as a stag, leapt clean over their heads and vanished into the dark.

Once again, Fionn was denied.

For many years, Diarmuid and Gráinne lived in hiding. They wandered from place to place, never staying long. Their love endured hardship. They bore five children, raising them on the road.

At last, weary of flight, they resolved to seek peace.

They came to Fionn's hall, their children beside them, and fell to their knees.

'Lord,' said Diarmuid, 'years have passed. Our suffering has been great. We beg your mercy.'

Fionn looked upon them – thin, weary, yet still proud. His heart softened.

'Rise,' he said. 'The feud ends this night.'

He welcomed them with a feast. For the first time in years, Diarmuid and Gráinne rested without fear.

Slowly, Fionn and Diarmuid rebuilt their bond adventuring, fighting and hunting side by side. Years later in the woods they came upon a monstrous boar, larger than any seen in Ireland.

'By the gods,' said Fionn. 'It is twice the size of any beast I have known. We must have it for our feast.'

The beast charged. Diarmuid met it with his spear, slaying it, but not before its tusks ripped his side. He fell, blood soaking the earth.

'Fionn!' he gasped. 'Your hands – bring me water. With water from your palms, I will be healed. Your gift from the Salmon of Knowledge can save me.'

Fionn ran to the river, filled his hands, and returned. But as he knelt, bitterness surged – the memory of betrayal, the image of Gráinne choosing Diarmuid. His hands trembled, and the water spilled through his fingers.

Diarmuid groaned, his breath faint.

The bitterness passed. Fionn leapt up, raced back to the river, filled his hands once more. He ran to Diarmuid's side. But it was too late. Diarmuid Ó Duibhne lay still upon the ground. The mightiest warrior of the Fianna was brought low not by blade or beast, but by love and fate.

The Lazy Beauty and Her Aunts

Long ago, in a small town in Ireland where the cottages leaned into one another like gossiping neighbours, there lived a weaver. She was the hardest-working woman for miles around. Day after day, season after season, her loom clacked and whirred from dusk till dawn. Reams of fine cloth piled up around her as she worked. She was said to produce more fabric in a month than three other women might in a year. Unfortunately for all her industry, all her aches and pains, all her early mornings and late nights she had been gifted the laziest daughter anyone had ever seen.

Her name was Anna. Anna was beautiful, with long hair like a river of gold, green eyes sparkling like glass and skin so pale that she must never have worked a day beneath the sun. And indeed she hadn't. From the time she was small, Anna had shown no interest in spinning or weaving, no matter how her mother coaxed or scolded.

If a broom needed to be lifted, Anna would groan as though it weighed more than an ox. If the fire needed tending, she would sigh and complain until her mother gave in and did it herself.

Most often, Anna could be found perched at the window seat, gazing dreamily into the sky. Neighbours passing by would shake their heads.

'A hurricane could come through, and the girl wouldn't stir!' they'd mutter.

The weaver tried every trick she knew. She promised her daughter little gifts if she would help. She threatened punishments if she refused. She scolded, bribed, cajoled and pleaded but nothing worked. Anna only grew as lazy as she was lovely.

The mother's only hope was that beauty could succeed where work had failed. If she won't weave her way to a good life, the weary woman thought, perhaps she can marry her way there instead.

One fine morning the chance she had hoped for came trotting down the lane.

A young prince, bright-eyed and handsome, was passing through their little town. As he passed the weaver's cottage, his gaze caught on the window.

There sat Anna, leaning her chin on her hand, her hair gleaming like a banner of gold in the sunlight.

The prince reined in his horse at once.

'My lady,' he called, 'you must be the most beautiful woman in all the land.'

Anna blinked, startled, but before she could reply, her mother bustled to the door. She had heard every word, and she knew better than to let her daughter ruin such a chance with some dreamy nonsense.

'She is indeed beautiful, my lord,' the weaver said, bowing. 'And not only that – she is the hardest-working girl you'll ever meet.'

Anna's mouth fell open in protest, but her mother silenced her with a glare.

The prince's eyes lit up. His mother, the queen, was strict and practical. She had always said he must marry a woman of good character, one who could work as well as charm.

'Is it true?' he asked eagerly. 'Can she spin?'

'Spin?' cried the weaver. 'She can spin three pounds of thread in a single day!'

The prince nearly clapped his hands with delight. His mother was an excellent spinner herself, and he knew she would be pleased to welcome such a kindred spirit.

'Would you honour me, fair lady, by visiting the castle this very day to meet my mother?' he asked, bowing low.

'Oh, yes indeed!' cried the weaver before Anna could form a word. She bustled her daughter into her best gown and chivvied her out the door.

Anna herself was uncertain. She had no great desire for queens and castles but the prince was very handsome and very polite, and she found she rather enjoyed the comfort of his carriage as it bore her away.

That afternoon, the prince presented Anna to his mother, the queen.

The queen sat upon her throne with a stern brow, her hands folded neatly in her lap. She appraised Anna from head to toe.

'Well,' she said at last, 'you are certainly very pretty. But beauty fades like morning mist. Tell me – what else can you do?'

Anna opened her mouth, but the prince rushed in, eager to help.

'She can spin three pounds of thread a day, Mother!'

The queen raised an eyebrow. 'Three pounds? That is most impressive. Then you will not mind proving it. Stay the night, my dear, and I shall have a wheel brought to your chamber. I will be glad to see such skill with my own eyes.'

Anna curtsied, her hands trembling.

That night she sat before the wheel in her chamber, her eyes filling with tears. Try as she might, the fibres broke again and again. By midnight she had not made a foot of thread, let alone three pounds.

'Oh, stupid Anna!' she sobbed. 'Why didn't I listen to Mother? Why didn't I work harder? Now I shall ruin everything!'

From the shadows of the room came a voice: 'What is the matter, pretty girl?'

Anna gasped. A woman stepped into the lamplight – an ugly old witch, her hips so enormous she waddled from side to side.

'Don't be afraid,' said the witch. 'I am a kind one. My name is Cailleach Cromáin Mhór – the Old Woman of the Great Hips. Now, tell me your trouble.'

Anna poured out her story between sobs.

'I have to spin three pounds of thread by morning, and I cannot do it. If I fail, the queen will never allow me to marry her son.'

The witch smiled. 'Then let me spin it for you. Only promise me this: when your wedding comes, invite me to it. No one ever invites me anywhere, and I long to dance at a feast.'

Anna agreed at once. Relieved, she lay down upon the soft bed, and the steady whir of the spinning wheel lulled her to sleep.

When she awoke in the morning, a pile of the finest gossamer thread lay at the foot of her bed. The witch was gone.

'Oh, thank you, kind witch!' Anna cried.

The queen was astonished when she saw the thread.

'This is the finest spinning I have ever seen,' she admitted. 'But spinning is not the end of the task. You must now weave it into linen. Stay another night, and tomorrow I will see your work.'

That night, the queen had a loom placed in Anna's chamber. Anna tried until her fingers ached, but the threads tangled and broke. At last, she wept again.

'Stupid Anna! Please, kind witch, help me!'

In answer, another figure stepped forth – a second witch, dressed in purple, with feet so large and hairy they stuck out from under her gown.

'Who are you?' whispered Anna.

'I am Cailleach na Coise Móire – the Old Woman of the Great Feet. My sister came to you last night. Why do you cry, child?'

Anna explained her plight.

'Well then,' said the witch, 'I shall weave it for you. Only promise that you will invite me to your wedding.'

Anna agreed. Once again she fell asleep, and in the morning she found a heap of the finest linen, neatly folded.

The queen examined it and could not hide her amazement.

'This is marvellous,' she said. 'But there is one more

task. Tonight you must make this linen into garments. If you succeed, you may marry my son.'

Anna trembled when the linen was carried to her chamber. She did not even attempt the work this time. She sank to her knees and prayed aloud.

'Please, kind witches, help me one last time! Come to my wedding, and I will do anything for you.'

A third voice answered, and into the room stepped another witch, clad in green, her nose long and red as a beetroot.

'I am Srón Mhór Rua – the Old Woman of the Great Red Nose,' she said with a grin. 'My sisters told me of you. What is it you need?'

Anna explained, and the witch laughed. 'That is no trouble. Sleep, my dear. By morning, the garments will be ready.'

And so it was. When the queen saw the delicate baby clothes, she clapped her hands.

'Wonderful! Your first child will be dressed in splendour. Anna, you may marry my son. Preparations shall begin at once.'

Anna and the prince were overjoyed. Within a month the castle was filled with banners, musicians and guests. True to her promise, Anna had made certain the three witches were written on the guest list.

She saw them sitting at the back during the ceremony – one with great hips, one with great feet and one with a red nose. They looked very odd among the lords and ladies, and Anna had to bite her lip to keep from laughing.

At the feast, the witches drank and danced until they grew merry. At last they came forward to the high table. Anna's heart pounded – would they reveal her secret?

But they only smiled and offered their congratulations.

'Do you know my bride?' asked the prince politely.

'Oh yes,' said the first witch. 'We are her aunts. I am Cailleach Cromáin Mhór.'

'What an interesting name,' said the prince. 'What does it mean?'

'It means Old Woman of the Big Hips,' she replied cheerfully. 'From long years sitting at the spinning wheel.'

The prince chuckled and turned to the second.

'And you, dear lady?'

'I am Cailleach na Coise Móire,' she said. 'Old Woman of the Big Feet – from standing at the loom all my life.'

The prince laughed outright and turned to the third.

'And you?'

'I am Srón Mhór Rua,' said the last, 'Old Woman of the Big Red Nose – from bending close over my sewing for many years.'

The prince and Anna could not help but laugh together.

'I don't want to end up with hips like that,' Anna whispered, giggling, 'or big feet, or a red nose.'

The prince squeezed her hand. 'Fear not, my love. You shall never need to sew a stitch again.'

And with that, the feast went on, and Anna vowed that she would be a good queen one day and work hard to take care of her people, although perhaps she would leaving weaving to someone else from now on.

The Lazy Beauty and Her Aunts

The Twelve Wild Geese

Long ago, in old Ireland there lived a great queen. She was blessed, or so everyone said, with twelve strong sons. Each boy was handsome, lively and gifted. She loved them all dearly. And yet, in her heart, she longed for something. Twelve sons were a great gift but was it too much to ask for just one daughter?

Night after night she looked out of her chamber window at the falling snow – the castle full of noise and laughter from the twelve boys running, shouting and tumbling. The energy that had once given her so much joy was now giving way to a terrible sadness.

One night, gazing at the moonlight on the snow, she whispered a terrible wish: 'I would give all twelve sons for a daughter – a daughter with raven-dark hair.'

The words had barely left her lips when the window burst open. Snow whirled into the room like a living storm, and through it stepped a witch. Her eyes glittered like ice.

'What a wicked wish that was,' the witch hissed, her voice sharp as frost. 'So wicked that I shall grant it. You shall have the daughter you desire, but the moment she is born, you shall lose every one of your sons.'

Before the queen could take her words back, the witch vanished in a swirl of snowflakes, leaving the room cold and still.

The queen's cry of 'No!' echoed through the chamber.

For days she tried to convince herself it had been a dream. She clung

to her sons, hugging them until they wriggled away in annoyance.

'What's come over you, Mam?' the youngest asked as she tried to smother him in kisses.

'Nothing, darling … nothing at all,' she said, though her face was pale.

But when certain smells made her stomach turn, when weariness pressed down on her bones, when her dresses grew tight around the waist, her dread grew heavier. She knew the signs. She had felt them twelve times before. She was with child.

She clung to hope. Perhaps the witch had lied. Perhaps she would have another son and nothing would happen. But as the months passed and the bump swelled beneath her gown, her terror grew.

She followed her boys everywhere, fearing that at any moment they would vanish. When her labour began, she locked them in the highest tower with guards at the doors, hoping somehow to protect them.

That night a child was born to her with a shock of raven hair. The cries of a baby girl filled the chamber. As the sound echoed around the stone walls, the air turned icy. A storm of snow roared through the halls. From the tower came shouts of alarm, then silence. When the guards forced open the doors, they found only a heap of clothes, twelve white feathers and an open window.

The queen looked out of her own window and screamed. Clearly visible flying against the night sky were twelve white geese.

For a year, the castle mourned. Riders scoured the land but found no trace of the boys. The queen loved her daughter fiercely, but grief sat in her heart like a stone. She swore the girl would never learn the truth, for what good would it do?

But secrets scurry through castles like mice. In time, the princess, now grown tall and fair with raven hair, heard murmurs of the twelve brothers she had never met.

She went to her mother, her eyes burning, 'Is it true, Mother? That I had twelve brothers who vanished when I was born?'

The queen wept. 'It is true. And it was my fault, child. My wicked wish.'

'Then I will find them,' the princess said. 'I will not rest until I do.'

'I forbid it,' cried the queen. 'The world is too dangerous. Stay here, I beg you, you are the only child I have left.'

But the princess's resolve was iron. That night, while the castle slept, she slipped away with nothing but her cloak.

For a year she wandered. She crossed tangled forests, swollen rivers, hill, valley and dale. She slept under hedges, in tree hollows, her cloak her only shelter. She desperately asked every villager, every traveller, any passing person, if they had seen twelve wild geese.

Most only shook their heads.

At last, deep in the woods, she came upon a lonely cottage. Exhausted, she crept in, hoping for a warm bed. The door creaked open under her hand. Inside was a long table set with twelve plates, twelve knives, twelve spoons. Twelve bunks lined the walls. Her heart leapt. 'Hello?' She searched all over the cottage but it was empty. Feeling disheartened she curled up by the fire and allowed sleep to take her. She woke at the sound of rustling. Night had fallen and twelve geese were flying in through the window. The moment their feet touched the floor, they became men.

'Are you my brothers?' she cried.

The eldest, tears in his eyes, embraced her. 'Sister, you've found us.'

She clung to each of them in turn, her heart swelling with joy. 'Come home with me,' she begged.

'We cannot,' said the eldest. 'By day we are birds. At night we are men. We are bound by the witch's spell.'

'Then I shall beg the witch to free you,' said the princess. 'I would give my life to see you restored.'

Snow swirled suddenly in the doorway. The witch appeared, her cloak of frost trailing behind her.

'That was a selfless vow,' she said. 'So I will give you a chance. If you wish to break the curse, you must weave twelve shirts of bog-cotton for your brothers. Until the task is done, you must utter not a word, nor a laugh, nor a tear.'

The witch vanished, leaving the cottage silent.

The princess returned to her mother's castle, mute. Each day she walked the bogs, gathering armfuls of white cotton. Each night she spun and sewed, her fingers raw.

Her mother begged her to speak, but she pressed her lips shut. Laughter bubbled in her throat at times, tears at others, but she bit them back. Silence was a prison heavier than she could have imagined.

Three years passed. She finished eight shirts, then nine. By then she had become a young woman. Most thought her strange in her silence and gave her a wide birth but even at a distance her beauty rang out like a bell.

One golden afternoon, while she worked in the courtyard, a young prince rode in. She noticed the gleaming copper hair, the amber eyes, the deft lines on brow and jaw. Her pulse quickened.

'Forgive me, lady,' he said, dismounting. 'I am a stranger here. May I rest a while?'

The princess inclined her head, her hands never ceasing their work.

He asked her questions, but she gave no reply, only gestures. Instead of cooling his admiration, her silence inflamed it. By evening he was bewitched.

'Come with me,' he said. 'Be my bride.'

The princess hesitated. Could she bring her task with her? She reasoned that bog-cotton grew everywhere. She nodded.

The next day they were married in the prince's kingdom.

The prince adored his mute bride, but his stepmother, the dowager queen, did not. Jealous and cruel, she spat, 'She is no princess. A lowly weaver, nothing more!'

Every time she saw the girl bent over her shirts, she sneered.

When the princess bore a son, her joy was boundless and there was contentment for a time. With renewed strength she worked at the last shirt. Only one sleeve remained, everything was going to be alright. She started deciding on all the things she wanted to say to her prince, all the things she would ask her brothers. Ha! Her little baby would have twelve uncles. Was there a luckier boy anywhere, she wondered?

One night the stepmother crept into the chamber. She lifted the infant from his cradle and flung him from the tower window. Below, a wolf prowled and caught the child in its jaws. Then the queen smeared blood on the cradle and across the sleeping princess's mouth.

In the morning she raised a scream. Guards burst in to see the damning scene, 'The witch has devoured her own child!' the queen cried.

The princess shook her head frantically but could not speak. She clutched the unfinished shirt to her chest as they dragged her away.

In the dungeon, she sewed by torchlight, her tears dripping but never falling, for she knew if she wept the spell would fail. At dawn the guards came. She had only a few stitches left.

They marched her to the gallows. The prince sat pale and broken, his stepmother triumphant. The people jeered.

On the scaffold, the rope was lowered around her neck. With trembling fingers, she tied the last knot in the final shirt.

'Stop!' she cried, her voice ringing across the yard. 'I am innocent!'

At that moment, a roar of wings filled the air. Twelve geese swept into the courtyard and landed. Their feathers melted into flesh and twelve young men stood before all.

'Our sister will not die,' said the eldest.

From the crowd padded the wolf. It laid a baby gently at the princess's feet and changed into the witch herself.

'You have proved yourself worthy,' said the witch. 'Your silence, your labour, your love. Your brothers are restored. Your child is returned. And as for you' – she turned to the

prince – 'shame on you for doubting your wife. It was your stepmother who cast the lie.'

The crowd roared in fury. Guards seized the wicked queen.

The princess at last gathered her son in her arms. She sobbed freely, her first tears in years. Her brothers lifted her high, and the people cheered until the very stones of the castle shook.

The Gardener's Sons

There was once a mighty king who ruled over all of Ireland. He was a wise and just man, loved by his people, but one winter he fell gravely ill. His physicians tried every herb, every potion and every remedy known in the land, yet nothing brought him relief. Days passed, then weeks, and still the king remained pale and weak, lying upon his bed while his council fretted and whispered about the kingdom's future.

One morning, as the first light of dawn crept through the tall windows of his chamber, the king gazed out across the royal gardens. They were a marvel to behold – lawns perfectly trimmed, fountains dancing in the sunlight and marble statues of Ireland's heroes. Yet what made the garden truly magical were the plants. Every corner contained something unusual: trees with silver leaves, flowers that glowed faintly at dusk and fruits from distant lands that no one had ever seen. The king, a lover of rare flora, sighed with longing.

Absentmindedly, he plucked an apple from a small tree that grew just beneath the window. The apples were tiny and delicate with skin as red as roses, a gift from the distant lands of Peru. The king bit into one, savouring its sweetness. At once, a warmth spread through his chest and he felt energy return to his limbs. Jumping from his bed, he laughed aloud, 'This is it! I have found the cure for my sickness!'

From that day forth, the king ate an apple each morning and with every bite, he grew stronger and healthier. But soon a problem arose. One night, as the moon hung low over the gardens, a large, luminous bird descended from the sky. Its feathers shone like burnished gold, and it moved with a grace that seemed almost otherworldly. It plucked an apple from the tree and flew off silently into the night.

The king, enraged, called for his chief gardener the following morning. 'I will not have my precious apples stolen! You must guard this tree night and day. If that bird dares come near, shoot it down!'

The gardener bowed deeply. 'Fear not, Your Majesty. My three sons are the finest archers in all Ireland. Whoever is on watch tonight shall protect the apples and bring down the bird.'

That night, the eldest son took his place in the orchard. He leaned against a tree, bow at the ready, yet before long, the warmth of the night and the gentle sway of the branches lulled him to sleep. The bird arrived, golden feathers glinting, and snatched an apple. The boy woke only as it flew away, helpless.

The next night, the second son stood watch. Determined not to fail, he remained alert, yet when the bird swooped in, his hands shook, and his arrow missed its mark. Another apple was lost to the magical creature.

By the third morning, the king's face was red with fury. 'This is intolerable! I warned you to bring it down!'

The gardener, distraught, fell to his knees. 'Sire, forgive me. My youngest son is swift and sharp as the wind. He will not fail.'

That night, the youngest son took his post. He paced the orchard, eyes never straying from the tree, bow strung and arrow nocked. When the golden bird descended, the boy released his arrow in a single, precise motion. There was a clear thunk and the bird cried out in surprise. It flapped its wings once, dropping a single feather as it escaped into the sky, and was gone before the boy could draw again.

The king hurried to the window, still scowling. 'Well? Did you kill it?'

The boy held out the feather. 'Sire, the bird has flown, but it dropped this as it went. Look!'

The king gasped. The feather was unlike any other, twelve inches long, gleaming with the purest gold. 'By all the saints! This is marvellous!'

He took the feather into his hands, turning it over again and again. 'Anyone who can bring me the golden bird, dead or alive, shall have half my kingdom!'

News of the king's proclamation spread like wildfire. The gardener's eldest son, eager and ambitious, set out immediately. He didn't even stop to eat, tearing chunks out of a loaf as he went. On the edge of an ancient forest, a fox with eyes bright as amber emerged from the undergrowth.

'Excuse me, sir,' said the fox, bowing his head politely, 'might you share a morsel with an old fox?'

'Out of my sight!' the eldest son

snapped, kicking the fox away. 'I have no time for beggars!'

The fox's eyes narrowed. 'Ah, you seek the golden bird, do you not?'

The boy's eyes widened. 'Do you know where it is?'

'Perhaps,' said the fox, 'but those who show no kindness will find nothing. Fairies down the path may help, but they do not favour the rude.'

The eldest son, impatient and proud, strode off without another word. Days passed, and he returned home empty-handed, discouraged and defeated.

The second son, hearing of the bird, embarked on his quest. Like his brother, he reached the old forest and was accosted by the fox, 'Might you share a morsel with an old fox?'

'You're no concern of mine,' he said, and hurried onward. Weeks later, he too returned without the bird, disappointed and weary.

At last, the youngest son set out. Unlike his brothers, he was humble and generous. When he came to the old forest, he shared his meal with the fox. 'Here, take this,' he said, offering a large chicken leg. 'And if you know the way to the golden bird, I would be most grateful.'

The fox's eyes gleamed. 'Ah, a wise and kind boy! Hold onto my tail, and I shall take you to Spain, where the bird resides in the palace of the King of Spain.'

The boy clutched the fox's tail, and in a swirl of wind, they soared across fields, rivers and mountains until the spires of the Spanish palace gleamed before them.

'Now,' said the fox, 'I will distract the guards. You must sneak inside and find the golden bird. Beware the halls – they are many, winding, a maze. But stay true, and you shall succeed.'

The fox darted between guards, biting at their heels and causing a great commotion. While the palace erupted in chaos, the boy dashed into the marble corridors. He passed through hall after hall, finally reaching a grand chamber at the far end. On a tall, gilded table perched the golden bird inside a pristine white cage. Beside it lay three apples, one with a single bite taken.

A small man in flowing robes stepped forward. 'Who are you, and what are you doing in my palace?'

'I am but a gardener from Ireland, my lord,' said the boy, bowing low. 'I mean no harm. I seek only the golden bird, for it has stolen from the orchard of my king.'

The little king, eyes narrowing, examined

the boy. 'You would brave my palace for this bird?'

'Indeed,' said the boy. 'My king offers half his kingdom to any who can bring him the bird.'

The little king chuckled. 'I cannot part with Santiago, my friend. But for your courage, I shall give you two golden feathers from his wings. One for your king, to placate him and one for you, a reward for your honesty and bravery.'

The boy thanked the king profusely and tucked the feathers safely in his satchel.

'Now,' said the fox, 'hold tightly. But first, you must share a portion of your reward with me, for I guided you here.'

The boy's face fell. 'One of them is for the king. Tell you what!' And the boy snapped one of the feathers in two. 'Half each?'

'Deal!' said the fox with a gleam in his eye. 'Onward!'

In another whirl of wind, the boy returned to Ireland. He delivered half the feather to the king, who was disappointed but perked up measurably when the boy told his tale. The king arranged to exchange a box of apples each month for a feather, ensuring the golden bird's safety and a steady supply of magical fruit.

In time the boy sold his half feather for a great fortune and built a small cottage with a flourishing garden of his own. There, he lived peacefully, remembered as the clever, humble son who dared where his brothers failed and found that honey really does catch more flies than vinegar.

The Children of Lir

There was once a king who lived long ago but his story has been told so many times it seems only yesterday. His name was Lir. He was venerable and most thought him wise and wise he was, at least most of the time.

He adored his children; Fionnuala, Aodh, and twins, Fiachra and Conn. To him they were the image of perfection and indeed the image of his wife. A familiar frown here, a recalled smile there. But these joyous recognitions were bittersweet. His wonderful wife had died shortly after birthing the twins. The pain had been almost unbearable but Lir focused on his love and duty to his children.

After many years as widower, Lir began to feel lonely. His children were growing up and soon his precious birds would fly the nest. What would he do then? He decided it was time to re-marry.

Unfortunately for Lir, wisdom deserted him when confronted with beauty. Aoife of Aran was known to the court, she was sister of Lir's late wife after all, but none had ever seen her. Tales of her beauty were sung across Ireland but nothing could have prepared them for Aoife. If only Lir had been able to look past the sweeping brow, the full lips, the cascading raven hair, he would have seen that her nature was cold and dark as a bog. Ambition bubbled in her always. When word reached her of Lir's intent to marry she rode for the castle at once. She charmed Lir, which wasn't hard, and they were married in a fortnight.

She tolerated her new husband but she loathed his children. Aoife had never been the maternal sort and annoyance prickled at her whenever she saw Lir with them.

After one particularly trying afternoon where Lir had had the children sing to them, Aoife stormed off to her bed chamber. She glared into her mirror, 'Those children,' she hissed, 'they have stolen his heart. Am I not his new bride? They've had years with him! If not for them, all his love would be mine.'

From that night, her thoughts turned dark.

She began to feign illness, claiming the noise of the children worsened her condition. Lir humoured her but would not send them away. The sound of their music still drifted through the corridors, bright and carefree. Aoife's jealousy grew until it burned like a fever.

On the hottest day of summer, she came to Lir in his study, where he sat over scrolls and letters.

'My husband,' she said, her voice like syrup, 'you look weary. Let me bring you a cup of wine to cool your blood.'

He smiled, grateful for the kindness. The wine was cold and spiced with herbs and something of Aoife's own concoction. The sleeping draft took effect almost at once. His eyelids drooped, and his head fell heavy upon his arms.

'Sleep well, my husband,' she whispered, stroking his hair. 'When you wake, you'll be free of those children.'

She left him there and went to the children's chamber. They stirred sleepily as she entered.

'Up, my darlings,' she said, 'Your father sleeps. Come, let us bathe in the lake, the day is too fine to waste indoors.'

Fionnuala frowned, 'Why does Father not come with us?'

'He is tired, would you deny him his rest?'

Reluctantly, the children followed her down to the shimmering lake. The sun beat hot upon the reeds, dragonflies flickered above the surface. 'In with you,' said Aoife with a thin smile, 'The water will cool your skin.'

Laughing, the children waded out into the shallows. Fionnuala splashed her brothers, and their laughter echoed across the still water. Then Aoife raised her hand, and in it glimmered a wand of rowan wood tipped with silver.

She spoke words no mortal should hear. A flash of blinding white engulfed the lake. When the light faded, four white swans floated upon the water, their eyes wide with terror.

'What has happened?' cried Fionnuala, her voice half-human, half-song.

Aoife stood upon the bank, her face triumphant. 'I am skilled in the old magic, children. You will wear these forms for nine hundred years – three hundred upon this lake, three hundred on the Sea of Moyle and three hundred more upon the Isle of Glora. Only the sound of a Christian bell shall break your curse.'

'Why?' cried Aodh, flapping his new wings in despair. 'Why would you do this?'

'Because your father is mine and mine alone,' Aoife said coldly. 'Enjoy your long years upon the water.' And with a laugh that chilled the air, she

turned and rode away.

When Lir awoke the castle was silent. He searched every room, calling his children's names. 'Fionnuala? Aodh? Fiachra? Conn? Where are you, my darlings?'

At last he heard Fionnuala's voice, faint and echoing across the water. 'Father, we are here! Look to the lake!'

He ran to the shore and saw four swans gliding toward him. They began to chatter over each other and Lir thought he must be dreaming or mad.

'Father, it is us,' said Fionnuala. 'Aoife has cursed us. We are lost to you.'

Lir fell to his knees, tears streaming down his face. 'My children, my beloved ones, what has she done?'

He rushed back to the castle, rage lending him strength. 'Aoife!' he roared. 'Wife! Witch!'

Aoife appeared at the top of the stairs, feigning innocence. 'Yes, my husband?'

'What curse have you laid upon my children?'

She smiled, serene. 'Do not weep, Lir. I have freed you from their hold. Now you may love only me.'

Something inside Lir broke. 'You are no wife of mine,' he said. 'You are a serpent.' He banished her from his sight forever, cursing her.

He returned to the lake. Day after day, year after year, he sat by the water, speaking to the swans, listening to their music. He built no new castle, took no new queen. When he died, he was buried upon the lakeshore, so his spirit might keep watch over his children.

The swans wept until their songs became part of the wind.

Three hundred years passed, and the swans grew

weary. When the time came, they flew north to the Sea of Moyle, where the waters raged between Ireland and Alba. There they suffered greatly, beaten by storms, frozen by snow and battered against sharp rocks. Fionnuala sheltered her brothers beneath her wings in winter and comforted them with lullabies in the dark.

Another three hundred years crawled by and they flew westward to the Isle of Glora. The waters there were mercifully calm, the air gentle. They sang each morning to the rising sun and each evening to the stars but their hearts were heavy with longing for a world that had long since changed.

At last, one dawn, as they floated upon the still water, a sound reached their ears, strange and sweet: the chime of a bell.

'What is that music?' asked Conn.

'It is the sound Aoife spoke of,' whispered Fionnuala. 'The end of our sorrow!'

They followed the sound to a small stone church upon the shore. There stood an old monk named Caomhóg, who watched in wonder as four white swans came gliding across the lake, singing with human voices.

'Holy saints,' he murmured, 'what miracle is this?'

Fionnuala spoke, her voice trembling with hope. 'Good father, we are the children of Lir, bound by a curse these nine hundred years. The sound of your bell brings us near release. Please, ring it again!'

The monk hurried inside and rang the bell till the rafters shook, but when he returned, the swans were unchanged. Their wings drooped in despair.

'Do not grieve,' said Caomhóg gently. 'Come into my house. You shall rest by my fire and eat from my table.'

That night, the swans lay by the hearth, their feathers glimmering in the firelight. Caomhóg fed them honey and barley and prayed beside them. But word of the singing swans spread across the land, reaching the ears of the King of Connacht.

'Such wonders belong not to a hermit,' the greedy king declared. 'They shall adorn my castle.'

He rode to Glora with his men and descended on the humble church. Peering through the window he saw the four swans resting by the fire.

He burst through the door, demanding, 'Give me those birds, monk, or I shall take them by force!'

'You shall not,' said Caomhóg firmly. 'They are under God's protection.'

The king shoved past him, knocking over a pail of holy water. The water splashed across the swans and at once their feathers fell away. In their place lay four frail, ancient humans, their faces lined with nine centuries of sorrow.

The king stumbled back in horror and fled the church.

Fionnuala gathered her brothers in her arms. 'At last,' she whispered, 'we are human again. But our time is short. Father Caomhóg, baptise us, that we may rest with our kin.'

The monk, weeping, baptised each of them in turn. When the last prayer was spoken, the siblings lay still.

Caomhóg buried them together in one grave, Fionnuala in the middle, her brothers on either side, as they had slept upon the sea. That night he dreamed of four white swans rising toward the sky, their wings glistening as they flew higher and higher, until they vanished into a radiant light.

And so the children of Lir were at peace, reunited with their father and mother beyond the tides of time.

But even now, when the wind blows over the western lakes of Ireland, people say it carries the echo of their sorrowful song.

Pronunciation Guide

Aengus Óg	*Ayn-gus Oh-g*
Ailill	*Ayl-illl*
Aillén mac Midhna	*Ayl-layn mock Meen-nyah*
Áinle	*Awyn-leh*
Alba	*Al-bah*
Anna	*Onn-ah*
Aodh	*Aey or Aeeh*
Aoife	*Ee-fah*
Aran	*Are-an*
Ardan	*Ar-dawn*
Balor	*Bal-or*
Benandonner	*Ben-an-donn-er*
Birog	*Bir-ohg*
Bol Sherca	*Boll Sher-kah*
Bres	*Breass*
Cailleach Cromáin Mhór	*Kayl-okh Krom-awyn Woe-er*
Cailleach na Coise Móire	*Kayl-okh nah Kush-eh Moyr-eh*
Calatin	*Kal-at-in*
Caomhóg	*Kway-vogue*
Cathbad	*Cah-bud*
Cian	*Kee-an*
Conchobar Mac Nessa	*Kuhn-khoor Mock Nyeass-ah*
Conchobar	*Kuhn-khoor*
Conn	*Konn*
Connacht	*Kun-nokht*

Pronunciation Guide

Conor Mac Neasa	*Kon-ur Mock Nyea-sah*
Cormac mac Art	*Korm-uk mock Ea-rt*
Culann	*Kul-enn*
Cumhal Mac Art	*Koo-yl Mock Art*
Cú Chulainn	*Coo-cull-in*
Dagda	*Dhay-dah*
Daire	*Dawy-reh*
Danu	*Dahn-uh*
Deichtine	*Jeykht-en-eh*
Deirdre	*Deeyr-dreh*
Diarmuid Ó Duibhne	*Jeer-mid Oh Dwee-nah*
Diarmuid	*Jeer-mid*
Dub Sainglend	*Dhoo Sayn-gleand*
Dónal	*Doh-null*
Éire	*Air-eh*
Eamhain Macha	*Owyn Makh-ah*
Emer	*Eem-er*
Eochaid mac Eirc	*Okh-ee Mock Eirk*
Eochaid	*Okh-ee*
Ériu	*Ayr-yiu*
Ethlinn	*Eh-linn*
Fedlimid mac Daill	*Fey-li-mee Mock Deel*
Ferdia	*Fir-dyah*
Fergus mac Róich	*Fer-gas Mock Roh-ick*
Fiacha	*Fee-ah-khah*
Fiachra	*Fee-ah-kh-rah*
Fianna	*Fee-yn-ah*

Finnbhennach	*Fin-van-ock*	Morrígan	*Morr-eeg-an*
Finnegas	*Finn-aayg-as*	Muirne	*Mooyr-neh*
Fionn Mac Cumhaill	*Finn Mock Oo-yl*	Muirthemne	*Mwir-heam-neh*
Fionn	*Finn*	Naoise	*Nee-shah*
Fionnuala	*Finn-oo-lah*	Niamh	*Nyeev*
Fir Bolg	*Fir Bul-eg*	Nuada	*Nuw-adh-ah*
Fomor	*Fum-oar*	Oisín	*Ush-een*
Fál	*Fawl*	Samhain	*Sow-yn*
Gamal	*Gom-al*	Setanta	*Set-an-tah*
Glas Gaibhnenn	*Gloss Gaiyn-enn*	Sreng	*Srang*
Glenna	*Glea-nnah*	Srón Mhór Rua	*Srown Woer Ru-ah*
Glora	*Glow-rah*	Staffa	*Sto-ffah*
Goll mac Morna	*Gull Mock More-nah*	Tailteann	*Taylt-enn*
Gráinne	*Graw-nyah*	Tory	*Toe-ree*
Labhraidh Loingseach	*Lauw-ree Luyng-shack*	Tuatha Dé Danann	*Tu-ha Jay Dann-yn*
Leabharcham	*Lauw-er-kham*	Tír na nÓg	*Tier Na Nogue*
Leane	*Lyehn*	Uisneach	*Ish-nekh*
Liath Luachra	*Lee-ah Lookh-rah*	Una	*Oon-ah*
Liath Macha	*Lyah Mock-ah*		
Lir	*Lyr*		
Lugh	*Loo*		
Láeg	*Law-egg*		
Mac Roth	*Mock Ruh*		
Macra	*Mock-rah*		
Maeve	*Mayv*		
Mag Tuired	*Moy Thir-ah*		
Maigne	*Myah-nhyn-eh*